THE TALE OF *Tiger Lily*

A NOVEL

JILL FEATHERSTONE

Tiger Lily

Tellwell Talent
www.tellwell.ca

ISBN
978-0-2288-3921-7 (Hardcover)
978-0-2288-3920-0 (Paperback)
978-0-2288-3922-4 (eBook)

To my daughter Arianna, who was with me
from the beginning and whose belief in me and
Tiger Lily never wavered, not even once.

To my husband Kevin, who held me up
and supported me through the seven years
that it took me to write this tale.

To my father William E. Ferland "Lum," who served
as a leader of Misipawistik Cree Nation for a quarter
of a century and whose humility, integrity, and
leadership inspired many attributes that I write about.

Special thank you to Kristen Hamilton for
your guidance, encouragement and wisdom;
and to Amelia Travis for helping me break
through my barriers of resistance. You both were
instrumental in the completion of this book.

And lastly, to "all my relations." Tiger Lily was written
in a way that would blend a little piece of each nation
into her unique fictional culture, but more importantly
she was written for the young Indigenous reader,
so that they could see a character just like them
portrayed so majestically in mainstream culture.

TABLE OF CONTENTS

AUTHOR'S NOTE

We can all recall the story of Peter Pan, and the brief but profound interlude with the lovely and discerning Tiger Lily.

When we saw her last, the beautiful Native American monarch had been captured by the infamous Captain Hook, who had bound her wrists and ankles and left her on a rock to await the imminent doom of the rising tide. Hook taunted her to reveal the whereabouts of Peter Pan, claiming she would risk the fate of never making it to the "happy hunting grounds" if she were to die a death of drowning. Through it all, Tiger Lily remained silent, proud and brave that she refused to reveal the hideout of Peter Pan even as the tide rushed in and threatened to wash her away. It was in that precise moment that Peter Pan swooped in to battle the angry captain and rescue Tiger Lily seconds before drowning. He would return her to the safety of her eagerly awaiting father, Chief Great Little Big Panther, and the tribe would celebrate Peter into the night.

That was the last we saw of the noble Tiger Lily and we are left only to speculate how such a young lady could have been so selfless and brave. What images raced through her mind as she was near death? If we could go back to that night and listen to her thoughts, what tale would they tell?

Could it be possible that the stubborn pride we all saw was but a mask for despair, and her silence, but a plea to end it all? If we could go back and delve further into her mind, what if Tiger Lily revealed that she did not want to be saved that fateful night at Mermaid's Lagoon? That she did not want to return to her village and the emptiness that awaited her there? When the tide rose up and Captain Hook was threatening her with death, could it be that she welcomed it? The only way that we will ever know is if we travel back before the capture, before Peter, before Tiger Lily could ever foresee that such danger was looming in her future.

If you are as curious as I, let us allow Tiger Lily to take us back to the days before this fateful event, before she felt that silence was the only way to end her suffering. Let us hear the tale of Tiger Lily…

Part One

CHAPTER 1

Why Must We Grow Up?

Faster, run faster! A breathless Tiger Lily raced heedlessly into the forest, away from her father and the crowds of people rushing to console her. Tiger Lily had not run through the woods this quickly since she was a child. It seemed not so long ago, but long enough that running had become an unyielding task rather than a frolicking adventure. When she supposed she had run far enough, Tiger Lily leaned her arms against a tall fir tree and allowed her chin to drop to her chest, panting to catch her breath. *This is far enough!*

Tiger Lily brushed away the stray hairs that had come free of her precisely fashioned double braids that Grandmother exacted each morning. As far back as she could remember, Grandmother wove Tiger Lily's shiny black hair into two perfect braids down the side of her head. The braids were so tight that they would pull her large brown eyes into the shape of almonds and further accentuate her already high cheekbones.

Tiger Lily was an immaculate beauty who would capture the gaze of all who looked upon her. Her petite, slightly upturned nose was complemented by a luscious set of full lips and solid jawline. However, behind those almond eyes was a great sadness. Tiger Lily was often lonely; when Tiger Lily was barely of walking age, her mother had died during childbirth. Her infant brother did not survive. Since then, Tiger Lily was cared for by her overly protective father, Chief Great Little Big Panther of the Piccaninny Tribe, and her elderly grandmother.

Tiger Lily had no visual memories of her mother other than images she had created from her dreams and the stories she had been told of her mother's beauty and the near exact resemblance they shared. The only thing Tiger Lily had left of her mother's was an eagle feather that was gifted to her on her wedding day by her own father—that and the one memory she had of her mother braiding her hair. Tiger Lily could still feel the tenderness of her mother's touch and how careful she was not to pull her hair, unlike the coarseness of her grandmother. Getting her hair braided was the one ritual she looked forward to least each day. But the pain would dissipate as soon as she tied the band around her head that adorned her mother's feather. Somehow it gave her strength and comfort in the times she felt most alone.

Tiger Lily knelt before the large fir. The thought of going a step farther made her legs weak. This would be the place she would ask for forgiveness.

Tiger Lily was supposed to feel anguish and grief, yet she felt relieved. Just moments before, Tiger Lily had fled the crowd of people gathering around her, fearing that she would not be able to simulate the feelings of sorrow expected of someone who had just learned of the death of the man to whom she was betrothed. Tiger Lily was guilt-ridden for feeling this way and needed to beg forgiveness from the Creator.

As she was about to reason her case, her friend Nascha came bellowing through the woods. "Tiger Lily, I am so sorry, but it will be all right!" Nascha threw her arms around Tiger Lily's neck in an attempt to console her. Nascha had to reach up to hug Tiger Lily, not because Tiger Lily was tall, but because Nascha was so short. Nascha was kind, caring, and always cheerful—the perfect complement to Tiger Lily's reserved but sometimes brash demeanour. "I am sorry that Walking Bear has died and he was to be your husband. I am here for you if you need to cry. I will help to ease your pain," Nascha said, squeezing Tiger Lily into a hug.

"Nascha, please, I need to be alone. I can't be around anyone right now. Please," Tiger Lily affirmed in an attempt to mask her guilt with sincerity. She could not bear to look at Nascha; her feelings of remorse were growing stronger by the minute. She really did just need to be alone.

"All right, Tiger Lily," said Nascha, calm and composed. "I will let you be alone to grieve, but if you need someone, you know that I am here for you." Nascha gave Tiger Lily one last squeeze and disappeared back into the forest.

Tiger Lily watched her friend walk away and decided that she should move a bit further into the woods to pray to the Creator in solitude.

When Tiger Lily came to an airy clearing at the edge of the woods that overlooked the open sea, she did one last glance around to make certain that she was alone. Tiger Lily then fell to her knees once more to release all that she had been keeping inside.

"Dear Creator, please forgive me for what I have done. I have killed my future husband. It may have not been of my own hand, although it may have been just as well, as I had wished him dead on more than one occasion. But you see, now that it has happened I assure you that I never meant it—though I am not certain that even this may be a lie, Creator, because I would not wish him back."

She paused, thinking.

"Oh Creator, please forgive my selfish thoughts. I take it back; if he could come back, I would sacrifice my own happiness so that I may never again feel the shame that I feel right now. Walking Bear was a good man and would have made an honourable husband. I would have learned to love him and I would have accepted my role as his wife."

This declaration satisfied her. Tiger Lily stood up and boldly decided that she meant what she had said. No sooner had she turned around when Tiger Lily heard a crack in the bushes, which startled her.

"Who's there?" Tiger Lily called out. "Nascha, is that you? I thought I asked you to let me alone!"

"It is not Nascha," said a voice from behind the bushes. "It is I, Jerrekai." A young man stepped into the clearing.

Tiger Lily recognized him as the son of a quiet builder in the village. He was close in age to her, although she had never learned his name. In their tribe it was not customary for women to speak with men who were not their husbands or who would not be potential suitors. Since Tiger Lily was born into nobility, her suitors would be warriors or sons of warriors, and if necessary, sons of chiefs in neighbouring tribes. Builders and farmers would marry children of builders and farmers. Tiger Lily would never need to converse with men aside from her future husband and her father. If builders and farmers were needed, it would be the husband that would order the work—and that's just the way it was.

"I heard you in the forest and I didn't want to startle you as you were praying to Creator," explained Jerrekai.

Immediately Tiger Lily felt embarrassed. "You should have announced your presence, or at least had the decency to excuse yourself. But I guess that is too much to ask of a coward!"

"How do you know that I am a coward?"

"Well, you are not a warrior so that only leaves one to assume that you are a coward," Tiger Lily snapped. She could hear the brashness in her voice, but she felt the need to assert her nobility.

"Forgive me," Jerrekai interjected, "I meant no disrespect, and before I leave you alone, I would just like to say that I am *deeply* sorry for your loss."

As Jerrekai turned to walk away, Tiger Lily could have sworn she saw him snicker.

That night Tiger Lily tossed and turned, replaying the afternoon in her mind.

Why did I have to be so mean? she fumed at herself. *What must he think of me? A spoiled brat with no feelings for anyone other than herself? Is what he must have thought? Oh, why do I even care so much? He's just a builder,* she reasoned to herself. But it was no use. Tiger Lily could not sleep, distressed over her meeting with Jerrekai. She needed to make amends. She just couldn't go about having anyone think so ill of her, builder or not.

The next morning, Tiger Lily took her time as she walked down to the village. The sun had not yet fully broken through the holes in the clouds and the grass was still wet beneath her feet, but the village was already busy; chatter and laughter were amid the air along with the smoke from open fires in front of huts and longhouses. Unlike the nomadic tribes of the north, Tiger Lily's tribe were permanent settlers. Their village was nestled snug in a valley with only a hillside separating them from the raging seas. It was an opulent settlement, in which Chief Great Little Big Panther had to fight many battles to procure. Having been granted the honour of becoming chief at a very young age, hence the name "Little," Chief Great Little Big Panther was highly regarded in these parts, not only for his wisdom as a long-standing chief, but also for the wealth that the seas brought in. Chief Great Little Big Panther had earned the right to be the first to trade and therefore the first to benefit from the wealth of the other lands. This made him very proud and powerful, but at the same time, very cautious and protective. Chief Great Little Big Panther was feared by many, but when it came to the hand of his most prized possession, his only child Tiger Lily, Chief Great Little Big Panther was feared by all.

Nearing the village, Tiger Lily spotted Jerrekai all too soon. He was busy at work preparing poles for a longhouse. She watched him from afar as he shaved and lifted the massive poles to resurrect a roof. The muscles on his body were well defined, unlike the soft and slender-looking body of the fallen warrior that was to be her husband. Jerrekai was visibly strong and robust, undoubtedly from heavy lifting and working hard each day.

"Hello," said a familiar voice from behind Tiger Lily. Nascha startled Tiger Lily so much that she let out a little squeal. She quickly grabbed Nascha and pulled her down behind a thick shrub as Jerrekai looked around to see where that scream had come from.

"Nascha! Why are you always creeping up on me like that?" Tiger Lily scolded, crouched behind the bushes.

"Why were you spying on Jerrekai?" Nascha countered in a voice as sour as her look.

"I was not," Tiger Lily lied.

"Yes you were!"

She sighed. "Okay, I was, but it is not what you think. I just wanted to get a better look at him."

"Why?" asked Nascha with the same sour face.

Tiger Lily ignored her last question and peered above the shrubs in Jerrekai's direction. "Would you say he is handsome?"

"No!" exclaimed Nascha. "He is just a builder; he is not a warrior or the son of a chief, or even the son of a warrior. He is just Jerrekai. Why?"

"I don't know," Tiger Lily answered honestly. "I just think that maybe we've never really given him a chance. Maybe there is more to him than we know. I am curious to find out what it is."

"Okay, Tiger Lily, but I will tell you right now that you are just fishing for trouble," Nascha warned. "Your father will not like you poking your nose around Jerrekai—you know it and I know it."

Later that day, Tiger Lily followed Jerrekai as he walked to the river. She stood behind a tree and watched as he cleaned his body of the sweat of a full day's work. Tiger Lily had never noticed such nice features on a man before and was surprised that they could come from someone who was a common carpenter and not a feared warrior.

He is a mystery. She felt compelled to learn more.

The next evening after dinner, Tiger Lily followed Jerrekai once more, this time to the same clearing in the forest where he found her praying to the Creator days before.

Jerrekai sat on a rock and began to carve out what looked to be a flute. She watched in amazement as he turned a piece of old wood into a magnificent musical instrument. When he began to play a tune, Tiger Lily felt herself becoming more enchanted with each note he played. *Now is the time to announce my presence,* she thought, but her pride stopped her. Instead she waited until he played another melody before she tiptoed out of the area.

The melody played in her mind for days afterward. Each day she found her thoughts becoming increasingly infatuated with Jerrekai and her yearning to see him again.

"The tipi pole facing west is cracking," Father bellowed in his deep, always superior-sounding voice. Tiger Lily jumped at his sudden presence. "I am off to see one of the builders to—"

"I will go, Father!" she volunteered. Tiger Lily jumped up, smoothing her hair. She slipped on one of her prettiest shawls. Wasting no further time, Tiger Lily set out on the path to the village to find Jerrekai.

There he was like every other day, working hard building their homes. *How could I not have noticed him before?*

"Jerrekai," beckoned Tiger Lily in a voice much softer than she had used the last time they spoke.

Jerrekai put down the pole he was carrying. Tiger Lily could feel her face getting flushed and her heart beginning to race. Such a strange feeling was coming over her, feelings she had never felt in the presence of Walking Bear.

Tiger Lily cleared her throat to keep her composure, but before she could speak, Jerrekai cut her off. "Have you come to give me another tongue lashing?"

This comment rattled Tiger Lily and she immediately threw up her guard. "I am here on orders from my father. You are to come fix the pole outside our hut facing west. He is expecting you." Tiger Lily turned and walked away angry, although this time she did not know if she was angry at him for harboring judgement or at herself for yet again coming across as brassy and arrogant.

Jerrekai followed Tiger Lily, who was practically jogging in an attempt to keep ahead of him. It made her feel better to act as if he was following her yet she knew that he would be walking in that direction had she been ahead of him or not.

When they arrived, Jerrekai wasted no time getting to work on the west pole. He was working so fast that Tiger Lily feared she would lose her chance to speak to him if she didn't come up with something clever to say, although she was terrified to mess up yet another encounter. The only question she could think to ask was the one that had been in the back of her mind all week.

"Are you promised to anyone?"

Jerrekai looked at her in bewilderment.

"No, I am free to marry whomever I choose."

A smile came across Tiger Lily's face as he spoke those words.

"Not anyone I choose, of course. I mean I could not marry just *anyone*," said Jerrekai.

Jerrekai turned back to his work, but Tiger Lily had broken free of her fear and there was no holding back.

"I think people should be free to marry whomever they want," she boldly declared. "Do you?"

"No," Jerrekai answered, still working.

"Why?" asked Tiger Lily.

"Because they just can't," Jerrekai huffed.

"That's not a good enough answer."

Jerrekai stopped and looked down at Tiger Lily. "People cannot be free to marry whomever they want because people like big chiefs would be very angry if their daughters married nobodies."

"But I don't think you're a nobody," stated Tiger Lily, staring bold-faced into Jerrekai's eyes.

The conversation was teetering on dangerous grounds.

Over the next few days, Jerrekai and Tiger Lily spent more time together. Tiger Lily kept him company while he worked and Jerrekai continued to allow her to ask silly questions, and some days after work they sat by the water's edge and learned about each other's lives. It was getting easier for Jerrekai to open up to Tiger Lily, but some days when Jerrekai would try to get playful with Tiger Lily, she was always quick to remind him that she was the daughter of the chief—she would not run, get dirty, or try anything daring. So they would sit and talk, and sometimes walk.

At night, when the village was fast asleep, Tiger Lily lay awake replaying the events of each day in her mind. Infatuated with her blossoming romantic feelings, she could barely sleep, her body alight, tingling with excitement, imagining the sensation of what it would feel like to receive her first kiss.

The summer was coming to an end; the trees had lost all their leaves, the birds had already left, and the beavers had stored the last of their food. Tiger Lily awoke to pouring rain and crashing thunder. Her heart sank because she knew that Jerrekai would not be out building in the rain. She moped around her home all day. She did not know what to do with herself; the day was dragging on so slowly. Toward the evening she couldn't bear it anymore. She needed to see Jerrekai. She could not fathom the thought of spending all evening without seeing his face or hearing his voice.

Tiger Lily left in the rain to find him. When she stopped in at his hut, he was not there.

Oh how romantic it would be, she thought to herself, *if he were there waiting for me in the rain in our spot.* She ran in the rain through the puddles that had formed along the path. And when she reached the clearing, her heart thundered in elation.

There sat Jerrekai in the rain staring down at the raging waters below. He jumped when Tiger Lily put her hand on his shoulder. When he turned to face her, she looked so lovingly at him—so happy—and in that moment Jerrekai finally let his guard down. As the sun was setting and the rain beat down against them, Jerrekai embraced the beautiful Tiger Lily in his arms.

Their bodies were pressed so tightly together that Tiger Lily could feel Jerrekai's heart beating rapidly against her chest. She looked up into his eyes and before she had a chance to speak, his lips found their way to hers.

There on the cliffside with the crashing waves and booming thunder sounding its applause, Tiger Lily's heart exploded in excitement. She was in love. She did not care that Jerrekai was not a majestic warrior, and when her father realized how much she loved him, he would understand. He had to.

When Tiger Lily arrived home soaking wet, she was surprised to see her father still sitting up waiting by the fire.

"Father..." she began.

"Silence, Tiger Lily!" the chief interrupted. "Why were you out in the rain chasing after the builder's son?" He didn't give Tiger Lily a chance to answer. "I am the chief—I know everything that goes on in my village and I don't have to remind you that you are my daughter and you live by my rules."

"But I have fallen in love with him," Tiger Lily admitted, her head down. She feared the roar that would inevitably come next. This was a fight she was afraid that she may not win.

"I want him banished!" growled the chief. "Immediately!"

Tiger Lily fell to his feet. "Please Father, do not send him away. He is a good man, you will see, you just need to meet him. Please…"

"Off your knees!" the chief commanded. "No daughter of mine will grovel on the ground for a wood cutter."

Slowly Tiger Lily stood up, but she could not look her father in the eyes.

Chief Great Little Big Panther rested his hands on Tiger Lily's shoulders and gave her one last command. "I am setting sail tomorrow morning to trade with Chief Red Sky of the sea tribes. You will sail with me and I may consider allowing the boy to stay."

"Yes, Father," said Tiger Lily obediently.

Tiger Lily crawled into bed. Although the conversation had not gone as hoped, it could have been worse. She knew her father felt pleased with his ultimatum and she was well aware of his motives. He was initiating a meeting between Tiger Lily and Chief Red Sky's son, Calling Bull. Since the day that Walking Bear had fallen, there had been daily talks of who Tiger Lily would marry, conversations that would happen in every home in the village. It was only a matter of time before her father would bring it up. But Tiger Lily had her own plan. She would use this voyage to convince her father that Jerrekai was worthy of her hand.

Early the next morning before anyone was awake, Tiger Lily crept out of the house and hastily made her way to Jerrekai's hut. Outside, Jerrekai's father was already awake enjoying his tea by the open fire. Without a word he motioned for Tiger Lily to wait and he went inside to fetch his son. A tired Jerrekai emerged from the hut, his brows knitted together in puzzlement to see Tiger Lily standing there.

"Jerrekai, I don't have a lot of time," Tiger Lily began. "I told my father that we are in love and he wasn't happy. Please don't be alarmed," she added quickly. "He promised no harm would come to you, but in return I have to sail with him on a lengthy voyage this very morning."

Jerrekai stood in silence. Tiger Lily took Jerrekai's hand in hers. "Please tell me that you will wait for me. I love you and I know my father will come around. I need you to trust me. Please tell me that you will wait for me."

Jerrekai looked down at Tiger Lily's delicate hands and into her tear-filled eyes. "I will wait for you," he answered as he pulled her into his arms for one last embrace and gentle kiss.

As the tribe gathered at the shoreline to give Tiger Lily and the chief a grand send off, Tiger Lily could not take her eyes off of Jerrekai, who stood off in the distance. Even from afar she could see the uneasiness in his eyes. Tiger Lily could only hope that he knew her heart belonged to him and that she would not fall in love with the neighbouring chief's son. She waved goodbye one last time before her eyes were pulled to the canoes coming in over the horizon.

"The tribes from the north must be coming to trade goods," observed the chief. "It is late in the season for them to be out this far."

Tiger Lily paid little attention to them and returned her gaze to Jerrekai. She would see her love again in the new moon. But if she only knew what the north winds were blowing in, would she have stayed? Could she have stayed?

CHAPTER 2

When the North Winds Blow

The morning sky was dark and grey, and the rain and the winds roaring in from the north made the canoes bounce wildly as they sailed toward the mainland. It was apparent from the shape of their small birch bark canoes and the rough unkempt appearance of the occupants that they were traders from the tribes of the north. Their bodies were thick and pale in contrast to the tribes of the south, whose crisp, clean attire adorned their slender sun-darkened skin.

When the canoes docked, children and adults of all ages began to unload them. They were to stay for a fortnight to trade Arctic furs of caribou, polar bear, and moose in exchange for the precious treasures of the south.

The days felt longer with Tiger Lily gone. There was quietness in Jerrekai's life. The daily company and conversations came to an abrupt end and Jerrekai's smile had faded. Some days he would walk up to the clearing in the woods and carve instruments to pass time; other days he would sit on the rock and listen to the wind blow, hoping answers would come for the many questions in his head.

Today was one of those days. As Jerrekai sat on the rock asking the Creator for guidance, his meditation was broken by noise coming from the branches behind him.

Jerrekai clutched his knife and braced himself to see a bear, but instead a strange-looking northern boy with wild curly hair jumped out of the bushes with a spear in hand in pursuit of a jackrabbit.

After a few unsuccessful attempts to spear the skilful creature, Jerrekai could not contain his laughter anymore.

The wild-haired boy stopped abruptly and turned to see Jerrekai holding his belly in amusement.

"You are doing it all wrong," Jerrekai called out in between chuckles. "You will never catch a jackrabbit with a spear. Didn't your father teach you about the hunt?" Jerrekai felt compelled to help the poor young boy of the north who didn't know how to hunt. "You need to set a snare. Here, let me show you."

Jerrekai looked for a good piece of willow to cut free. He peeled back the layers of willow to produce strands that he quickly weaved together to form a snare, which he then tied to a short branch near the trail. The boy watched in silence.

"Here, you try," Jerrekai offered.

As Jerrekai handed over the knife and the willow to the boy, he gasped at a sudden realization. The young wild-haired boy was in fact a young wild-haired girl. "You're not a boy!" he exclaimed.

"Of course I'm not a boy."

"Then why are you hunting?" asked Jerrekai, still in shock. "Girls can't hunt!"

"No," she countered, "girls aren't *supposed* to hunt. It doesn't mean we can't." The wild-haired girl began to cut and fashion a snare just as easily as Jerrekai had. "And I know how to catch a rabbit! I was merely perfecting my technique. Didn't your father ever teach you that spearing a jackrabbit is the best practice for a hunter?"

She picked up her spear and headed back down the path, then called out, "I'll be back to check my snares in the morning!"

The next morning as Jerrekai was working, he found himself peering over his shoulder at the trail leading to the clearing. He had been so shocked by the girl who was hunting that he continued to think of her all night.

Finally at mid-morning he noticed the girl heading toward the trail. Quickly, Jerrekai set down his tools and went into the clearing after her.

"Why were you hunting?" asked Jerrekai, finally releasing the question that had been on his mind since yesterday.

As if the wild-haired girl was expecting him, she didn't bother turning around as she answered. "The same reason men hunt—to bring food to my people and for the rush I get when the animal goes down on the first hit."

Jerrekai was surprised with her candidness. "Is this some sort of new age thing in your tribe?"

"No, but I do it anyway as long as nobody knows," she revealed. "Anything I catch I give to my brother and he brings it in for me as his own."

"Clever," Jerrekai said, astonished.

"I could probably show you a trick or two," she teased.

Jerrekai smiled back at the girl, who behind all that wild curly hair was quite pretty. She had large round eyes with just a tint of sepia, a small button nose, and a wide grin that ended with dimples in her full cheeks. But it wasn't just the appearance of the girl that had him smiling. Her pleasant voice, her confidence, and her wit had Jerrekai feeling as if he already knew her.

Hours quickly passed as Jerrekai and the wild-haired girl wandered through the woods swapping hunting secrets, each always trying to top the other. She came from the north, she explained. She and her tribespeople were on their last leg of trading before returning home, and would sail away when the chief and Tiger Lily returned.

Come supper, they had talked so much that they forgot to hunt. Jerrekai, starved for the conversation that he had been missing since Tiger Lily left, invited the girl back to the clearing later that evening to show her something he had made.

The sun had already begun to set when Jerrekai finally finished the work he had neglected that afternoon. He rushed to the clearing without even a bite to eat, hoping that he was not too late. When he arrived, the wild-haired girl was nowhere in sight. Disappointed, Jerrekai turned, sat on the rock, and put his head in his hands.

"RHAAAR!" the girl yelled as she jumped up from behind the rock.

Jerrekai was so frightened that he stumbled forward in a failed attempt to flee.

The girl laughed at him. "Ahh, brave Jerrekai, how will you ever protect me from the wilds of this world?" she teased. "I think I will have to protect you...and hunt for you, and trap for you..." She laughed again.

Jerrekai smiled widely. He found her little games amusing and he was just happy that she had waited.

"I want to show you something," he said, pulling a handmade flute from his pouch. "This flute is different from the flutes carved from wood. It is made from the reeds of the sea."

"How did you acquire such a possession?" She looked at it curiously.

"I made it myself," Jerrekai professed. "When I was a boy, my uncle would take me salmon fishing on the Great Sea. Every now and then we would come across reefs that were shallow enough for us to see clearly along its bottom. Uncle would dive down and cut the reeds to make flutes for all the little children in the village. Since he has now passed, I decided that I would like to carry on this tradition. But this is the first one I've made. I'd like to practice a few more times before I start handing them out."

"I think it is spectacular," the wild-haired girl said with admiration. "I have clearly underestimated you," she added jokingly. "May I try it?"

"Yes," said Jerrekai. "Do you need me to show you?"

"Do I ever need you to show me?" she said, smiling.

The girl put the flute to her lips and began to play a melody that was unquestionably foreign. But for Jerrekai, it was the most enticing melody that he had ever heard. He stretched out in the grass beneath the stars and watched the northern lights dance wondrously to the music.

One by one, the next few nights would be more magical than the previous. Jerrekai continued to be amazed by the wild-haired girl and her adventurous spirt, and she in turn was always surprised with Jerrekai's knowledge of the world and ability to craft whatever he needed. Not a day went by that they would not laugh and play and tease and challenge each other, but they also knew how to be serious and offer praise when praise was due—though never far in the back of his mind was the beautiful Tiger Lily.

Jerrekai often found himself comparing the two. Tiger Lily seemed delicate and pure—handle her with care or you may break her, touch her and you may dirty her. There were things that she could not do and sometimes there were things she refused to do. Tiger Lily did not run and play like the wild-haired girl. She didn't long for mindless adventures and distractions. Tiger Lily was practical and reserved; she knew what she wanted and what was needed, whereas the wild-haired girl ignored the rules and questioned the unknown.

But in his heart, Jerrekai knew that Tiger Lily loved him. He was certain of that love just as he was certain that she would be back. The only thing he was uncertain of was the feeling that he had when he was with the wild-haired girl. He knew it couldn't be love, because it was impossible to be in love with two people. Whatever the feeling was for the wild-haired girl, he was sure it would leave when she did.

One afternoon as Jerrekai and the wild-haired girl were out on one of their adventures, Jerrekai found the answer that he had been seeking.

Up they went. It was a race to the top of the great sycamore tree. Jerrekai did not even try to let the wild-haired girl get a head start; she didn't need it. Once they reached as high as the branches could sustain, they sat in silence for several minutes to catch their breath. There they sat at the highest peak either of them had ever been, marvelling at the splendour of creation. All around them were treetops and meandering rivers, smoke from the fires in the tiny village below, and in the distance, mountains and valleys as far as the eye could see.

"Do you know the only thing that could possibly happen right now that could be more exhilarating than this?" the girl said to Jerrekai.

"What?" Jerrekai asked, eager to hear her answer.

"This," said the wild-haired girl as she leaned into Jerrekai and pressed her lips firmly against his.

What Jerrekai felt in that moment had far surpassed anything he had ever felt before. It felt as if all the breath had been removed from his body and replaced with a cold burst of fresh water. His body quivered with pleasure, and right there at the top of the world, Jerrekai knew that what he was feeling was love.

As the pair walked back to the village, giggling and holding hands, Tiger Lily was far from Jerrekai's mind. He was in love with the wild-haired girl; when he was with her, he could no longer think of anyone else.

But just when Jerrekai was enjoying the feeling of no longer struggling with the questions in his mind, he was suddenly halted when they came face to face with Nascha. He immediately let go of the wild-haired girl's hand and braced himself for Nascha's reaction.

Nascha walked up to the couple and without taking her eyes off Jerrekai, she said, "Jerrekai, may I speak with you in private?"

Jerrekai looked at the wild-haired girl. "I will see you this evening." Then he turned back to Nascha who had not taken her glaring eyes off Jerrekai.

"WHAT ARE YOU DOING?" Nascha yelled. "What is Tiger Lily going to say when she finds out you have a little girlfriend?"

"Nascha, you don't understand." He put his hands out, trying to calm her. "I care deeply for Tiger Lily, but you and I both know that she and I don't have a future together. I know she will be hurt, but she will be hurt either way. Her father wants me banished from the village and she's willing to risk everything for me. I can't let her do that."

"Oh, you sound so noble," Nascha sneered, expressing her disgust. "Please don't try make me believe that you are doing all of this for her."

"No," Jerrekai said. "But it is why I am letting it happen."

The two were silent for a moment, then Nascha said her final words. "It may be what's best for her in the end, but it won't prevent her heart from being broken."

Nascha walked away, leaving Jerrekai standing alone.

The evening air was cold as the winds blew fiercely. Jerrekai had been waiting for hours for the wild-haired girl to show up, and just as he was about to give up, she walked into sight. There was going to be no easy way to have this conversation and Jerrekai had no idea where he would begin.

"I was going to let you freeze here tonight," the girl said, "but I decided to come hear what you had to say for yourself. I know whatever it is, it is going to be unpleasant, so you may as well get talking so we can both get over it and move on."

Her forwardness made it easier for Jerrekai to just come out with what he had to say. Even though he did not feel like he was hiding anything because they were only friends, relationships as important as the one he had with Tiger Lily should have been talked about—yet he never spoke of her once.

"There is a person in my life—a girl, not the one that you saw, but another," confessed Jerrekai.

"Well, where is she now?"

"She went away with her father, the chief," he said, finally looking up.

The girl stood in silence. This was the first time Jerrekai had ever seen her speechless. As she tried to make sense of what Jerrekai had just said, he continued, "Her name is Tiger Lily, and we shared a secret relationship before her father took her away. He did not want us together. They set sail the day you arrived and she asked me to wait for her until she returned and I said I would."

Again there was an unfamiliar silence between the pair. The only sound was the raging winds that Jerrekai tried to ignore.

"I always knew in the back of my mind that she and I could never be together the way she wanted, and when I should have been falling in love, I was falling more into anxiety. Then you showed up and without effort or fear, I fell in love. I've never felt more happy and alive than I do now. But before you say anything, I don't want you to think that I fell in love with you because it was allowed. I fell in love with you because you are amazing. You are…"

The girl put her fingers on his lips. "Did anyone ever tell you that you talk too much?" She smiled. "Don't get me wrong, I'd like to hear you finish telling me how much you love me, but it's cold out here."

Laughing, they embraced in the night air, and as they walked back to the village the wild-haired girl thanked Jerrekai for his honesty.

Over the next several days, the north winds did not ease up and snow blanketed the ground. The songs of the magpies were gone and beavers too had disappeared from sight. No one had predicted that winter would come so early.

Word spread to the village that the weather had delayed the chief's return. He and Tiger Lily would not be able to travel until the northern winds settled; this early winter also meant that it would delay the wild-haired girl's departure.

Jerrekai did not know which emotion was stronger, his happiness or his relief. The only feeling that was certain was his affection for the wild-haired girl. He could not live without her; it scared him to think that the time for her tribe to sail back home was not far away. There was only one option left: When the day came that she would sail away, Jerrekai would sail with her and Tiger Lily would be set free to fulfill her destiny and marry her warrior. Jerrekai took great solace in knowing that the beautiful

Tiger Lily would one day find the same happiness that he had found.

There in the presence of both tribes, the couple joined together in marriage, solidifying their love for one another. The days that followed were filled with joy as the young lovers played all day long, made love each night, and frolicked in the bliss of knowing that they would never have to part. But among all the happiness and laughter, looming in the back of Jerrekai's mind was the reality that Tiger Lily would be back soon and they would have to leave the village.

Jerrekai made a promise to himself that he would not leave until Tiger Lily's return so that he could honour her feelings with the respect that she deserved. He may not have been a warrior, but he was no coward.

When the weather calmed and the boats could sail again, Jerrekai watched as the wild-haired girl bid her family safe travels. She vowed to stay on with him to await Tiger Lily's return and then the two would leave together.

The day came sooner than anticipated. As Jerrekai and his wife were out gathering feathers to make arrows, they were interrupted by a great eruption from the tribe. The chief had returned, and with him, his beautiful daughter Tiger Lily.

CHAPTER 3

The Winds Collide

The voyage out to sea seemed long and never-ending. Tiger Lily was anxious every inch of the way, feeling as though countless impediments delayed their voyage, and more than once she wondered if she would ever see home again. Mulling over the last few weeks, Tiger Lily was eager to get back to her handsome builder. How awful it was to be made to spend time with the anticipated Calling Bull.

Tiger Lily had been relieved that her father was not impressed with the man who was not yet a man. Chief Great Little Big Panther had such high hopes for this union, but he was clearly disappointed and the prospect of Jerrekai was suddenly looking up. Tiger Lily had taken every chance she could find to convince her father that Jerrekai would be a great provider and a kind husband. Toward the end of their journey Tiger Lily was near certain that she may have finally sold him on the idea.

As the boats neared the familiar islands, Tiger Lily's eagerness to see Jerrekai grew. She squinted until she could faintly make out the tufts of black smoke emerging from the treetops. Once the outline of the huts appeared across the skyline, Tiger Lily was ready to burst with anticipation. She could not wait to run into the arms of the man she loved and tell him that they could finally be together. Tiger Lily had never been so happy.

When the boats docked, Tiger Lily scanned the shoreline for Jerrekai, but he was nowhere to be seen. A wave of panic set over her but she quickly put it out of her mind. *He must just be lost in the crowd and will appear soon enough.*

While Tiger Lily and her father exited the boats, they were met by a procession of tribe members eagerly waiting to welcome them home. Tiger Lily filtered through the crowds of people, half-heartedly accepting their greetings, anxiously awaiting the appearance of the only person she could think of since she left. Then she heard a familiar voice call her name.

There stood Nascha with open arms waiting to embrace her friend. Tiger Lily waved to her friend and tried to keep going; she was so eager to find Jerrekai that she didn't notice the sombre look on Nascha's face, but she was halted when Nascha yelled, "Tiger Lily, come here!"

Tiger Lily walked over to Nascha who was waiting to embrace her. When she let go, Tiger Lily asked immediately for Jerrekai. She did not notice Nascha's concerning look.

"Tiger Lily, I have some bad news."

Immediately Tiger Lily's heart pounded in panic. "What is your news? It's not Jerrekai—he is not dead, is he? Nothing horrible has happened to him?"

"No, he is fine," Nascha assured her. "Nothing bad has happened to him. But..." She paused and put her head down. When she looked up, she put her hands on Tiger Lily's arms. "There is no easy way to tell you this..." She breathed deeply. "He's married."

In that one sentence Tiger Lily felt the breath ripped from her lungs. She stood there motionless, unable to stomach what she had just heard. She scanned the crowd for him, wishing now that he was dead if this news were true.

"What do you mean married? He can't be married... he loves me."

"Come, Tiger Lily, come, let's walk." Nascha pulled her friend away from the crowd. As they walked, Nascha filled her in about the canoes that came in to trade on the day she had left and that on one of the canoes was a young wild-haired girl who had won the heart of Jerrekai.

"I tried, Tiger Lily," Nascha said, trying to provide comfort to her friend. "I went up to Jerrekai and asked him why are you marrying her when you love Tiger Lily? He could only reply that it was something that he had to explain to you himself. I'm sorry, Tiger Lily."

Tiger Lily was in tears. She and Nascha sat by the tree line until the crowds of people cleared. "I have to see him. Once he sees me, he will know, and then he will remember his love for me. I have to see him!" she declared.

"Tiger Lily, wait, don't go!" pleaded Nascha. "They are married now."

She adamantly refused to believe that he was in love with this stranger. "He cannot love another the way he loves me. Their marriage can be undone and he can marry me. She is not even from our tribe. I am the daughter of the chief. He has to see me and then he will know."

Tiger Lily ran back to the village—she needed to find Jerrekai. She began to frantically ask the tribe members if they had seen him. But no one had. She ran to the area where she watched him build on so many occasions, but he was not there. Finally someone answered her. Tiger Lily spun around to see a small boy staring up at her pointing to a little hut in the corner of the village.

"Jerrekai is in his house, right over there. I just saw him and Miss Shakori go in there."

For the second time today, words had struck a blow worse than a weapon. Tiger Lily's palms began to burn and her whole body was tingling. But it was more than a feeling, it was a taste, and that taste was seeping through her body, up out of her chest, out of her palms, and up into her mouth. It was the bitter taste of betrayal.

Tiger Lily was again breathless. This was becoming too surreal. Tiger Lily had only just left for a short while, and Jerrekai already had a wife and they had a home.

As she stood frozen in front of their hut, Tiger Lily tried to process the thoughts that were throwing her mind into such disarray… *I feel like I'm the outsider, like I am intruding on their life, yet this is my life, he loves me and this is my home.* This couldn't be happening to her. *What is going on?*

Then Tiger Lily realized that she had an audience behind her. She could not bear to turn around and face the humiliation of everyone watching her, waiting to see what would happen. Everyone knew that she had loved Jerrekai and that he had married someone else. Tiger Lily didn't know if she needed to scream, or throw up, or faint…

And then it happened. Jerrekai came out of his hut and there they stood face to face.

"Tiger Lily," said Jerrekai with an uneasy pause, "I was hoping I would find you."

"You knew that I would be coming off the boat," answered Tiger Lily curtly. "Why were you not there if you were hoping to find me?" Her question came out as more of a scolding.

Jerrekai could not look her in the eye. "Tiger Lily, can we talk in private please?"

"Where?"

"Would you come inside?" he asked, finally looking up at her.

"No, I will not!" Tiger Lily said boldly.

"I understand." He looked down again. "Can we walk?"

"Yes."

Tiger Lily turned from the hut. The audience was at a standstill as they watched her and Jerrekai exchange words.

Side by side they walked in silence; she knew where she was going and so did he. They soon found themselves at the spot where they spent so many afternoons talking, exploring, and falling in love.

When they came to the clearing, Tiger Lily took her place on the rock in the same way that she had sat countless times before to watch Jerrekai do silly things to impress her, yet this time the smiles and laughter were replaced with silence.

But the silence was too much and Tiger Lily couldn't hold her composure any longer. "Well, speak! You wanted to talk to me!"

Jerrekai forced the courage to speak. "I can only say I am sorry."

Tiger Lily glared in his direction; this apology was not enough.

"I never meant to hurt you, Tiger Lily. I care about you a great deal and the last thing I ever wanted in this world was to hurt you. But…" Jerrekai closed his eyes to speak this last sentence. "I fell in love."

Tiger Lily turned away when she heard those words but Jerrekai continued, "You and I both know that we could never be together."

"But I think I finally have Father convinced!" Tiger Lily pleaded.

"Tiger Lily, you know that he would never fully accept me. To tell you the truth, I don't even know if I could have accepted myself. As much as I cared for you, I never felt worthy of your love."

Tiger Lily tried to interrupt but Jerrekai continued to speak. "This is not an excuse, it's the truth. When Shakori and I…"

"Don't you dare say her name to me!" Tiger Lily demanded. She was losing this battle and all her dreams were being destroyed.

Tiger Lily turned to walk away when Jerrekai make another gut-wrenching announcement. "I am leaving. We sail in the morning. I stayed only long enough to say goodbye."

Anger quickly turned into panic as Tiger Lily imagined how it would feel to never see Jerrekai again. "No, you can't!" Tiger Lily begged. "I'll never see you again!"

"Tiger Lily, I can't stay. I can't hurt you any more than I already have, and if I am here you will not be able to move on and you will not find the man who is right for you. I wished that man could be me, but it never was. Please understand," he said. "I do have love for you and you will always hold a piece of my heart."

"If you love me, why can't you marry me?"

"Tiger Lily, please," Jerrekai said in a solemn voice. "Shakori and I are connected at the soul, beyond anything that I could ever explain or anything that I ever knew I could ever feel. I want you to feel that love, Tiger Lily. But you won't feel that love until I have freed you from me."

Jerrekai gently wiped away the tears that streamed down Tiger Lily's cheeks.

"When you find this love, Tiger Lily, you will know and you will understand. I promise you will."

Jerrekai took Tiger Lily in his arms one last time and kissed her on the forehead.

Tiger Lily pushed him away. "I will never forgive you and I will never understand!" She ran off into the night.

The next day Jerrekai was true to his word—he and Shakori were packing up to leave. But Tiger Lily needed to get a glimpse of her. She needed to see who Jerrekai was leaving her for, and this would be her last chance.

Jerrekai had been called to the feast hall to say his formal goodbyes to the members of the tribe as his wife stayed behind to pack up the rest of their belongings. Tiger Lily hurried over to the hut, careful not to be seen, and slipped inside.

There stood Shakori staring blank-faced back at Tiger Lily. It appeared that she too had hoped to get a glimpse of the princess Jerrekai had loved not so long ago. The two stood in silence as they both took in each other's features.

Shakori was the first to speak. "I know who you are. You are Tiger Lily, and you are every bit as beautiful as Jerrekai described you to be, maybe more so." She looked down, seeming inadequate of her own beauty.

Even though this made Tiger Lily feel superior, it did not give her Jerrekai and she did not feel sorry. "Why did you come in between the love that he had for me? Have you no shame? Had you not known that he was in love with someone else? Had you not known he was to be married to me?"

"No!" cried Shakori. "I did not know, and when Jerrekai told me of you, he said that he could not marry you, as he wasn't the great warrior that your father wanted for you."

"Don't speak for my father!" Tiger Lily snapped.

"Jerrekai said he was common just like me."

"NO!" yelled Tiger Lily. "He was not just like you! You are a crazy-haired girl that is nothing and nobody and Jerrekai is a skilled craftsman and he was destined to be my husband, and now you've come in and ruined everything! Did you put medicine on him? Did you make him fall in love with you? I've heard stories of you girls from the north, is that why he is going far away from his family and from me, the daughter of the chief?"

"No," declared Shakori. "I love him and I would never trick him or hurt him or force him to do anything."

Deep down Tiger Lily knew that her accusations were false but she felt the need to hurt the girl in any way she could. Was there something she could say to make her leave? She looked around at all that should have been hers. *If only I had come back sooner. If only I had never left.*

In one last-effort strike at the wild-haired girl, Tiger Lily lashed out in fury, "I hope you know that he could never love you the way he loves me. You will never have beauty such as mine, and as the years age you, I will remain a beautiful memory that you will always be compared to. You stole him from me! You will never be happy with something that does not belong to you! I will always own his heart because I had it first and you are a thief! Thieves can never be truly happy with that which does not belong to them!"

Tiger Lily stormed out of the hut, hoping that the words she aimed at her rival pierced through her heart as hard as any arrow, to destroy the confidence the wild-haired girl had in her future.

As Tiger Lily walked away from the hut, she stopped briefly and thought about going back. But she didn't go back. The only comfort she could find would be in knowing that the wild-haired girl would be unhappy and maybe, just maybe she would go home…alone.

Though, later that morning Jerrekai and his new wife sailed off to begin their life together.

Tiger Lily went to their spot overlooking the water's edge and watched them sail away. She watched until their canoe vanished beyond the horizon. At that moment, Tiger Lily knew that she would never see Jerrekai again. She fell to the ground and cried. She cried all that day and mourned her loss. She grieved his departure from her life and cried until the breaths were gasping from her, and when she could cry no more, she got up off the ground, broken and defeated, and walked slowly back to her hut where she slept for two days.

Tiger Lily dreamed of being stuck in a swamp. It was cold and dark, and she was powerless to scream or to move. The darkness crept closer and sunlight and hope were nowhere in sight. She awakened with a scream. Tiger Lily's grandmother immediately rushed to her side and wrapped her in her arms. "Tiger Lily, what is the matter?"

Tiger Lily began to speak of her fretfulness.

"You must try to put Jerrekai out of your mind," Grandmother urged. "You were never meant to be his wife, nor were you meant for Walking Bear. You are Tiger Lily, named after the wild flower, which never grows in the same place twice—the flower which stands higher and more vibrant than all the other flowers in its midst. Someday you will find a good man to stand behind."

"But I am not content to just stand behind my husband the way Mother did," Tiger Lily argued. She knew it was wrong to speak ill of her dead mother who loved her so much.

"Tiger Lily, you may think that your mother just stood behind your father," Grandmother explained, "but what you don't realize yet—and what you may not see until you are much older—is that love is a partnership. Your father is in a position of great power and greater responsibility. Many lives depend on him and the decisions he makes.

Your father relied on your mother to support him, mind, body, and soul. His decisions were never made alone. Someday you will find love and you will know, for you will put his needs before yours and his happiness before yours, and he will do the same. And when you find this one, you will walk side by side through this life and you will stand behind him when he needs your support."

No sooner had Grandmother finished when Father came in and interrupted. "Tiger Lily, you must stay indoors—pirates are circling the North Mountain. I am off to Mollusk Island to warn Peter Pan!"

CHAPTER 4

The North Mountain

Tiger Lily lay nestled beneath her buffalo hide blanket watching the fire's embers float toward the ceiling of her hut, as if racing to the top, each one vying to climb higher than the next before burning out without ever reaching its destination.

Grandmother sat on a chair near the fire weaving strands of sinew in and around a circle-bent branch of willow, moulding a dream catcher to hang at the bedside of her heartbroken granddaughter.

"Why does Father worry so much about the white-skins' safety?" asked Tiger Lily, making no attempt to hide the tone of annoyance in her voice. "To me it seems that they are nothing but trouble."

Grandmother was a tiny woman with long grey hair and brown withered skin. Both her eyes and nose were turned down and her thin lips quivered each time she spoke.

"They come and they go," Grandmother said with her ever-present wisdom. "They have been coming for years on their boats and we welcome them because it is not our place to judge the unknown. We are all equal in the eyes of the Creator and each life, large or small, serves a purpose."

Grandmother paused as if to let Tiger Lily's young mind process the lesson. "The white-skins are not always completely without use." Grandmother smiled and gave a wink. "Each person we come across in life will always bring something with them, whether good or bad. But however you choose to feel about the white-skins, you must never forget that your father feels a great loyalty to Peter Pan."

It had been nearly four full seasons since Peter Pan and his band of young sailors arrived on their shores. But Tiger Lily remembered it as if it were only yesterday—after all, who could forget hair as orange as fire and skin as white as the clouds?

Peter was a white-skin who had come from across the Eastern Sea on a great ship decorated with a pirate's crest. He and his gang of Lost Boys, as he liked to call them, set up camp on the shores of the North Mountain in search of gold. Peter could not have been much older than Tiger Lily, though he had a way about him that added years to his young demeanour. Peter stood out from all the others and was clearly the leader.

Father was angered by the squatting of the intruders and set out to aggressively remove them from his land. However, Chief Great Little Big Panther's fury was no match for Peter's charm. With merely his words and his wit, Peter had not only convinced the fearless chief to let them stay, but had also procured protection against any tribe who would threaten their safety. What Peter had to offer in return was something that no other tribe had possessed, or even knew they wanted: gold.

The tribes of this vast land had only ever seen this yellow metal fashionably adorning the white-skins' fingers and sometimes decorating their necks, though it seemed that the white-skins were most pleased to carry this precious treasure around inside their pouches.

It was up on the North Mountain that Peter and his Lost Boys found an abundance of gold that had yet to be unearthed. In exchange for an alliance, Peter offered to teach Chief Great Little Big Panther how to pan for gold.

The chief was hesitant at first, as he found it amusing to watch the white-skins wade through the water violently shaking pans. But he quickly found out that the gold was highly sought after by explorers and easily tradable for goods. The tribe benefited greatly from this shiny rock and the chief quickly became the most well-known and highly regarded chief in the land. It was also how Peter came to be known as Peter Pan.

The wealth of gold and the partnership established between the two leaders provided an unfamiliar comfort to the young men. Peter and his Lost Boys settled on a nearby island known to the locals as Mollusk Island, which Peter nicknamed Neverland, "on account of the fact that they would never need to leave." Though as secure and wealthy as they were, Peter and his Lost Boys lived simple lives filled with frolic and freedom. They were happy and for the first time ever, they had a place to call home.

Most days were spent panning for gold because it had become such an enjoyable pastime. Peter had an unrestrained imagination and would often tell wild stories of pirate battles and faraway lands. Panning for gold even became a hobby of the chief, which was unusual, as duties such as these were customarily given to the women of the tribe, but the chief enjoyed Peter's company. Some days the chief and Peter's Lost Boys would not exhume a single nugget of gold because they would become engrossed in the tales told by their colourful storyteller. Those days would be spent sitting along the riverbanks listening with unremitting attention to the exaggerated tales told by an energetic Peter Pan.

It wasn't very long before Peter was a welcomed presence in the village and whose stories attracted the tribespeople to the campfire to hear about how the white-skins lived over the Great Sea. Though, the most interesting and probably the most poignant story of all was the story of how Peter Pan and his Lost Boys came to be on Neverland four seasons ago.

Peter's story began far away in a land called England, at London's Orphanage for Lost and Wayward Boys.

As a young boy barely able to see over the tabletops, this was also where Peter planned his first adventure… He would run away as soon as he was tall enough to jump from the second-story window.

The orphanage seemed no place for a child, as ironic as that may sound. It was musty, old, and colourless and run by nuns and priests who could almost be described the same. Children were forced to do manual labour when they became school-aged. Although they were given the necessities of life such as food, shelter, and clothing, they were strapped routinely when disobeying and deprived of the one necessity all children required in order to thrive: love.

Every boy in the orphanage longed for a mother. They longed for hugs, bedtime stories, and someone to be proud of their accomplishments. In the early years of the orphanage, a young nun would read stories to them—stories of Tom Sawyer and Huckleberry Finn, Oliver Twist and Peter's most favourite, *Treasure Island*. However, the older nuns in the orphanage reasoned that these "new age" stories were damaging to the children and gave the boys a false sense of hope. The young nun was no longer permitted to tell the stories and was soon removed from the orphanage. On her last night there, she gave them instructions to always be good boys and to never grow old, and gave each one of them a kiss on the forehead.

Peter never forgot the stories, even as the years rolled on. In fact, they expanded in his mind into theatrical tales that easily diverted his attention and kept him amused during rainy days and hours of endless pot-scrubbing. Peter would often get strapped due to his inattention being mistaken for defiance. But he could not help himself, as the characters in his mind were beginning to take on a life of their own.

One night as Peter lay in his bed, he heard soft whimpering. He propped himself up on his elbow and listened. A young boy three beds over was crying.

"Hey," Peter whispered. "What's wrong?"

The boy sniffed for a minute, composing himself. When he could finally speak, he said, "I miss my mother."

Instantly, the large room full of orphaned boys became silent. Not even a breath could be heard.

Peter sat straight up in his bed. "Mother?" he questioned.

"Yes," answered the young boy between sobs. Suddenly the boy's sobs were joined by another, and then another, and another, until the whole room was sobbing uncontrollably.

Peter jumped out of bed.

"Stop with the crying!" he whispered urgently. "The nuns will come in with their straps and they'll give us all something to really cry about."

Still, the boys continued to sob. The only way Peter could get any them to calm down was if he promised to tell them a story. So Peter chose the story of Oliver Twist, an orphan in London just like them who runs away to seek fortune and adventure. The story settled the boys and from that day on, and each night after, they would beg Peter for another story.

Every day as Peter swept and mopped and scrubbed, he would dream up stories that he could tell the boys at night. Then he would let loose the characters, who had spent the day blossoming in Peter's mind, and unleash a tale that would come alive in the imaginations of all the boys in the room. Some nights Peter would become so engrossed in his own tales that he would fly about the room leaping across beds enacting fight scenes and fleeing from thieves and vagabonds. But as much as the boys liked hearing the stories, and as much as Peter enjoyed telling them, the time was drawing near for Peter to leave on his own adventure.

When that day finally came, Peter's closest companions, the Lost Boys, decided they would follow. They would all claim their freedom together.

Each boy went about the day as usual, cleaning pots and folding linens, scrubbing floors, and getting strapped. When the sun's last rays disappeared from the skyline and nightfall happily set in, the boys lay stiff in their beds anxiously waiting for the facility to fall fast asleep. Minute by minute, the hours of the clock ticked on. Finally, Peter, followed by the group of boys, left their beds to begin carrying out their plan.

In hushed silence, they tied their bed sheets together from end to end until they formed a makeshift ladder. Peter tied one end to the bed post and then gently opened the window to toss the rest of it out the side of the building.

Just as the boys were about to embark upon their escape, a little voice from the back of the group broke their silence.

"I'm scared," said the little voice.

There stood the littlest Lost Boy, whose sobs had once woken the whole room and set Peter on his path to becoming a great storyteller. Knowing he could not leave the boy behind, Peter had to convince him in the only way he knew how—with a story.

"There once was a magical fairy named Tinkerbell..." he began.

Peter promised the little Lost Boy that Tinkerbell had come in and sprinkled invisible fairy dust on all of the boys which had enabled them to fly, so that if they fell, they would not get hurt. But they would need to hurry because the fairy dust would not last long.

Peter was first out the window and down the ladder. One by one, the Lost Boys followed Peter's lead and shimmied down the ladder after him. Once their feet hit the ground, there was only one place left to go: the ocean. Only a ship could take them as far away from the orphanage as possible.

It was early morning when the boys finally reached the ocean docks. They were hungry and tired and beginning to question whether they had made the right decision. But just when the idea of freedom was beginning to lose its lustre, they couldn't believe their luck. A captain of a large ship was recruiting deck hands to sail on a long voyage with them. Mr. Smee, the short, stalky, nearly bald-headed captain's chief mate spoke of lands far away full of gold and riches, and how it could all be theirs if they chose to sail with them and work on the ship to earn their keep.

It did not take much to convince any one of the Lost Boys to board the ship; Peter and the others almost ran over each other trying to get aboard. Adventure had found them and at last they were free!

The ship was headed by an unpleasant man named Captain James, whom they only referred to as the captain. He was tall and slender with black curly hair that fell to the middle of his back. He wore a long velvet coat and a large brimmed hat that, along with his hair and curly moustache, concealed most of his face.

The captain took an instant disliking to Peter, whose leadership of the Lost Boys challenged that of the captain's. Peter was immediately separated from the other boys and made to work as a servant for the captain and his men.

Their voyage would take them to remote islands and new lands to dig for treasures and pan for gold, sometimes for months on end. Most times there would be very little gold, and other times there would be none—and the less gold they found, the more enraged the captain became. The captain would throw men overboard if they got in his way during one of his rages, especially on the days that he and his men would overindulge in the ale.

Occasionally just for amusement, the captain would have the men bind Peter's feet together and hang him upside down over the side of the ship as they sailed along, hoping to attract mermaids. The Lost Boys were powerless to aid their leader, yet the whispers of "Tinkerbell, please guard Peter with your fairy dust" pleaded silently in their eyes.

The captain's thirst for gold was becoming so great that in a fit of anger, he instructed his men to start pirating and looting other ships. Only when treasure was brought aboard did the captain's perfervid mood lessen, but this would not last long. His hankering for gold was intensifying.

Peter had put the boys in a dire situation, and it was now up to him to get the Lost Boys out of it. He would need to devise yet another escape plan, but this time it would take more skill and cleverness than the first.

In the wee hours of the morning, Peter and his Lost Boys struck while the pirates were in a dead sleep. They climbed quietly out of their sleeping corners and crept up onto the ship deck. There lay the comatose pirates, strewn about the deck asleep where they fell after a night of drinking and celebrating another successful plunder.

One by one, the Lost Boys lifted the pirates up over the mast of the ship and threw them overboard into the cold, murky waters below.

Mr. Smee, who was not partial to liquor, heard the commotion and woke to see the Lost Boys tossing the last man overboard.

"Captain, Captain!" Smee cried. "Wake up, Captain! Wake up! It's those boys! And they're throwing the crewmates over! Oh my!"

In only his night clothes and sword in hand, the captain stumbled out of bed and ran to the ship deck to see only Peter and his boys on board the ship, then to the edge where he saw all his men flailing about in the water, crying out for help. Howling in anger, he raised his enormous sword above his head. The only thing that stood between the captain's sword and Peter was an empty ship deck.

The captain lunged toward an unarmed Peter as the boys watched in paralyzed fear. The moonlight danced about the captain's blade as he swung at Peter, narrowly missing him with every blow.

The captain's skilled fencing expertise was of little aid against Peter's youthful speed and agility. Peter flew almost acrobatically, seeming to gain energy as the captain grew only wearier. When the captain grew fatigued from the chase, Peter saw his opportunity to strike. He leaped from the mast he was perched on and grabbed the sword from Mr. Smee's grip, knocking him flat on his rear end. In one swoop Peter swung the heavy blade at the captain.

A collective gasp echoed across the deck as it seemed that Peter had missed his target. But then the captain's sword dropped to the ground as his now free hand gripped his left arm.

The captain stood in shock as he stared at his left arm that no longer had a hand attached to it.

The ship was silent as everyone stared at the hand, on the deck. Realizing what happened, the captain lunged toward his hand to retrieve it, but he was too late—Peter kicked the severed hand swiftly into the crocodile-infested water before the captain had a chance to pick it up. Into the dark water his pale hand sunk, below the waves and out of sight.

"Come, boys! Let's help him find his hand!" yelled Peter. He and the Lost Boys advanced, backing the captain into the corner.

"Captain, down here! Take refuge!" Mr. Smee called out from below. Mr. Smee had cut a lifeboat free and was motioning for the captain to jump.

The captain awkwardly climbed over the side of the ship to make his escape, but before he did, he headed a final warning to Peter.

"I will take my revenge," the captain sneered, holding his bloody stump, "if it is the last thing I do."

The captain jumped into the waiting lifeboat and floated into the darkness with Mr. Smee.

Peter and his Lost Boys cheered and embraced Peter as they sailed away with the captain's ship and all his gold. Once again they were free. They had conquered the ship and could go anywhere in the world they wanted.

"Where shall we go, boys?" Peter said, victorious.

"Away from pirates and away from orphanages!" one boy chirped. They all cheered in agreement.

"Then we shall head west!" declared Peter, grinning from ear to ear.

And so it was—they unfurled the sails and headed west. Their voyage would eventually bring them to the North Mountain and then to Neverland where they would settle permanently. Here they lived in peace and safety, far away from the captain, who had notoriously become known as Captain Hook, after the hook that was in place of the hand that Peter had cut off.

Fuelled with rage and revenge that was beyond anything anyone had ever heard of, Captain Hook dreamed of the day he would conquer Peter and feed him limb by limb to the crocodiles. He was ruthless and cold, and quickly became the most well-known and most feared pirate in all of the oceans. The only person he trusted was his long-time companion Mr. Smee. On Captain Hook's instruction, Mr. Smee oversaw the voyage to find Peter, who had become just as famous as Captain Hook for his bravery.

Stories of the great battle that occurred between Peter and Captain Hook spread quickly throughout the land. The surviving pirates who were thrown overboard the ship that night would retell their own accounts of what happened in bar rooms and parlours. Some claimed that Peter could move so fast that he seemed to fly, his fiery red hair burning bright as he darted about the ship. Some claimed that he single-handedly fed Hook's hand to the crocodile himself. It was not known what happened to Peter after that night, but they only knew that he did exist, for what else could explain the madness that fuelled Captain Hook's arduous search?

Finally, after years of searching, Captain Hook located the region of the Piccaninny Tribe, where Peter was rumoured to be.

Mr. Smee tirelessly questioned the locals and bargained most of their gold trying to find the hideout of the white-skin they called Peter Pan. The location was the same each time: Neverland. But where was this Neverland that the people spoke about? No one could tell them. The only man who knew was Chief Great Little Big Panther. Eventually Mr. Smee stopped asking about Peter and began asking about the chief.

It did not take Mr. Smee long to learn that the chief of the Piccaninny Tribe was a powerful man, who was feared by all and who feared no one. His loyalty to Peter Pan was revered and second to only one—his precious only child Tiger Lily.

Mr. Smee knew what he had to do.

CHAPTER 5

The Happy Hunting Grounds

Alone in his intricately carved birch bark canoe, Chief Great Little Big Panther paddled to Neverland Island. The sun had long since disappeared from the sky and had been replaced by a large iridescent moon that provided just enough light to guide the chief to the desolate shores; the only sounds that could be heard were the audible blasts of waves crashing against the rocks.

When the chief arrived, he pulled his canoe up onto the island shores and followed a beaten path into the woods. He continued on in the dark along the meandering creek until he reached the drop where the stream spilled into a pool of water surrounded by tall caves and cascading waterfalls. There, on a small rock cliff, Chief Great Little Big Panther pulled out his flute and started to play an enchanting tune.

In the early days of the Lost Boys' arrival, Peter often sat near the falls playing this melody. He told stories of how many of the pirates claimed to have seen mermaids bathing beneath waterfalls, and they would play "The Mermaid Lullaby" in hopes of luring them to the surface.

This same lullaby was the one that Peter instructed the chief to play if he ever needed to summon him. The chief would need only to make his way to the water, play the tune, and wait.

Peter and his Lost Boys were believed to have built their homes in the trees of Neverland. The exact whereabouts were unknown to all but the chief, and the entrances to their elaborate dwellings were so well hidden that even he had trouble finding them alone.

Halfway through the chief's song, Peter emerged from the woods; his Lost Boys stayed hidden, never too far behind.

"Great Chief, my friend, what brings you here at this hour?"

"I have news that Captain Hook and his men have been circling the island," he warned. "His men outnumber yours by twenty...but mine outnumber his by one hundred." The chief's voice was strong and echoed against the rocks. "They have offered gold to whoever can lead them to you."

The Lost Boys emerged from the trees, though Peter did not break his gaze with the chief. "Thank you, my friend, for this warning. It was brave of you to come here alone on this night to warn us."

"If you need to seek refuge in my village, my warriors will protect you," the chief continued. "That sea scum will not have a chance to get near our shores."

"That is very kind of you," said Peter. "But I think it best if we stay here. I cannot bring trouble to your people."

"Hiy, hiy." The chief nodded. "My men will be ready. We will keep watch for your smoke signal." The chief turned and walked back down the path to the creek that brought him in.

When Chief Great Little Big Panther finally returned to his own shores, daylight had begun to brighten the sky. He had hardly made it out of the canoe when he was alerted to high danger. His best warriors were racing on horseback in his direction.

After her nightmare, Tiger Lily was wide awake. Father had still not returned from Neverland and Grandmother was fast asleep. She knew her father warned her to stay indoors but Tiger Lily just could not lie awake in her torment. She figured that a little bit of fresh air would do her good and might help her sleep.

She tiptoed quietly out of bed, still in her night clothes, and ventured out of the hut and into the darkness. There was only one place she could think of to go, and as if in a trance, Tiger Lily made her way in the dark to the clearing in the woods. All alone in the night, Tiger Lily watched the waves dance in the moonlight; their ever-constant sounds as they rushed up on the shore always brought her comfort.

When the darkness began to fade and daybreak was near, Tiger Lily knew it was time to get back to the village. She needed to return before her father could find out she disobeyed him.

To her relief, Father had not yet returned and Grandmother was still asleep. Tiger Lily slid quietly into bed and beneath her warm blanket. The fresh air was exactly what she needed, and she closed her eyes and fell back asleep for a second time that night.

No sooner had she fallen back asleep when she was awakened by cold, callused hands against her satiny skin. A large, rather smelly white-skinned man was standing above her, staring toward her bare legs that had come exposed beneath her nightdress. Tiger Lily tried to scream but her call was quickly muffled by the man's large hand.

"Well looky what we 'ave ere. I thought I'd 'ave ter scour this ere whole village, but cha led us right to yer." The smelly man smiled, exposing several missing teeth. "Must be me lucky day!"

"Aye! Ya don't have time to be messin' er-round. Tie 'er up and let's get goin'!" This command came from a smaller white-skin just as dirty and with more facial hair than the first.

The man bound Tiger Lily's mouth with a handkerchief and tied her hands behind her back.

I led them straight here, Tiger Lily thought, tears springing to her eyes. *This is all my fault.*

She had just been saved from an attack on her innocence, but she also knew that her fate had yet to be determined. Tiger Lily was flung over the shoulder of her captor and carried out of the hut as her poor grandmother lay bound and gagged on the floor. Grandmother's tiny eyes welled with tears as the small white-skin gave his commands.

"Tell yer big chief that if he wants to see 'is daughter again, he can bring Peter Pan to Cap'n 'ook. He'll be waitin' fer 'im up at Mermaid's Lagoon. Dead or alive… I don't think the crocs'll care how they get their dinner."

Tiger Lily's eyes widened. Mermaid's Lagoon, one of the islands in the archipelago that she was instructed never to go to. She and Nascha had snuck off there in a canoe years ago; Tiger Lily felt a lightning strike of fear bolt through her chest the first time she laid eyes on the giant island where the haunting sounds of the rumored mermaids wafted eerily into her ears. They had turned around, fear in their hearts, and never came back.

The small pirate let out a chuckle and then gave his final directive. "And if 'e brings an army, I'll send 'is little princess to 'er happy huntin' grounds sooner than he'd wish, but not before we 'ave our way with 'er."

Then they were gone, into the night with Grandmother left alone on the floor near the weakening fire where just minutes before she lay in a peaceful slumber.

Swift Horse, the newly appointed head warrior, jumped off his horse to convey the news to his leader. With distress in his voice he revealed the unsettling news to the awaiting chief.

"Elder Niikamich was awakened by the sounds of cries coming from your hut! When he entered, your mother was tied up on the floor so weak she could barely speak."

Chief Great Little Big Panther instinctively broke his attention at the sign of trouble to his family, but before he could run off toward his hut, Swift Horse jumped in front of him with his hands raised.

"Chief! Tiger Lily is gone. The pirates have taken her to Mermaid's Lagoon. If we bring our men, they will kill her."

The chief ignored the threat. No one, not even pirates, could threaten the safety if his greatest treasure.

Within minutes, dozens of canoes lined the shores ready to set sail. But before getting into his canoe, the chief handed his flute to his trusted warrior. "Take this flute to Mollusk Island. Follow the creek to the falls and play a tune. When Peter shows himself, tell him of this news."

Swift Horse sailed in the opposite direction of the others, paddling more swiftly than he had ever done before.

In those fleeting moments that Peter was in danger, it never dawned on the chief that he could be the target. The chief was the only one that could give Captain Hook access to Peter Pan.

This was Captain Hook's master plan. He knew that by circling the waters, the great chief would want to warn Peter. He played on their friendship—and once the chief took the bait, the pirates came in for their attack. Captain Hook anticipated that Peter and his Lost Boys would always be on the lookout. Peter had eluded him for so long that he would never reveal himself so foolishly.

No one followed the chief to Neverland; instead, the pirates used this diversion to allow them the time they needed to carry out the one sure-fire plan to capture Peter Pan once and for all.

When Swift Horse reached his destination, he brought the flute to his lips and began to play. No one emerged from the trees. He played another song again, louder and quicker than before, and still no one came out.

Swift Horse scanned the trees in desperation. Finally he dropped the flute at his side and with his hands cupped to his mouth, called out, "PETER PAN, THE CHIEF HAS SENT ME FOR YOU. ARE YOU THERE? HIS DAUGHTER HAS BEEN KIDNAPPED!"

Suddenly Peter appeared on the opposite side of the creek bed.

"Chief Great Little Big Panther sent me here to find you," Swift Horse called out to him. "He gave me this flute to summon you. The pirates have kidnapped Tiger Lily. They have taken her to Mermaid's Lagoon. The chief has gone to look for her," he finished, almost out of breath.

Peter turned back toward the woods behind him and let out a sharp whistle. The Lost Boys emerged from hiding and surrounded the two men.

"The beautiful Tiger Lily has been captured by Captain Hook," Peter called out. "We can't waste time!"

A great uproar was let loose among the boys and they began to holler like men charging into battle. Working together, they immediately started to unearth their ship from its hiding place inside a massive cave, while Peter boarded the canoe with Swift Horse to lead the way to Mermaid's Lagoon.

Tiger Lily had only ever heard of Captain Hook in stories told by Peter and corroborated by his Lost Boys. Coming face to face with him now, she could see clearly that every fragment of the stories was true. Captain Hook was indeed dark, hostile, and gruff. He was quite tall, though not as large as her father, but one could see that he was equally as confident.

After taking her from her hut, the pirates brought Tiger Lily aboard their ship and transported her to the remote Mermaid's Lagoon. Once there, they carried her down into a grotto where the tide had not yet risen. Cold, damp, and tired, Tiger Lily showed no signs of weakness or fear. She could see that her stoic behaviour was unfamiliar to the pirates, which confused them and caused their normally confident attitude to feel eerily tense. This silence intensified the echo of the waves splashing about in the darkened cave dwelling.

The quiet seemed to irritate Captain Hook, who finally walked over to Tiger Lily. "Let's make this easy on everyone and spare the bloodshed," he snarled. "Where is Peter Pan's hideout?"

Tiger Lily sat upright on the rocks, restricted from movement. She looked the captain straight in the eyes. "I will tell you nothing," she declared with not so much as a blink.

He grimaced. "Well then, we will have to do this the hard way...well, hard for you, easy for me." He looked over at Mr. Smee and growled, "Tie her to the rock!"

Mr. Smee and the two captors hurriedly began to wade Tiger Lily through the water toward a large rock which jetted out in the middle of the lagoon.

"Young miss," Mr. Smee whispered in Tiger Lily's ear, "please tell the captain what he wants to hear... He will kill you!"

Tiger Lily turned away from the pleading little man, offering only silence as her answer.

Mr. Smee shook his head and sighed, then gave the instructions for the two pirates to tie her to the rock.

"Eventually the tide will come in," Captain Hook began, his voice echoing off the cave walls, "and if you do not reveal the whereabouts of Peter Pan, you will never make it to your happy hunting grounds." The captain turned to give his final order to his men. "Leave her tied to this rock until she tells us what she knows." Then he leaned into Mr. Smee and pompously uttered, "Leave her here even after she does."

Mr. Smee trembled as he watched Hook walk away. He pleaded to Tiger Lily with his eyes but she turned away and refused to look at him again. The pirates paddled away, leaving Tiger Lily alone on the rock bound so tightly that there was no escape.

It was believed in the Piccaninny Tribe that if you were to die by drowning, your spirit could not go on to the spirit world, and that it would remain in limbo for eternity. But Tiger Lily could not find it in herself to fight. With each passing minute, she dared death to come for her. With Jerrekai gone, her mother gone, the hurt she had caused her grandmother and the burden she would become on her father if she could not love a warrior, she could not find the will to live any longer.

If I go back to the village, I'll be faced with humiliation over losing Jerrekai to that outsider. I will have to live the rest of my life with the agonizing grief of knowing that he is living each day in her arms instead of mine. Tiger Lily fought back tears. The more time that passed, the more her thoughts tormented her. *I will not live to be the laughing stock of the village, to be known as the princess who was left behind for a nobody. I do not need their pity.*

There was no one left for her to love and she would be all alone forever. This was agony she was not ready to face. She would wait for the tide to take her away and Jerrekai would hear of the news and would have to live with the guilt of knowing that he could have prevented her demise. If he would have stayed true to his promise, she would be alive and happy. Tiger Lily had made her decision. If death was to be her fate today, then she embraced it.

As the tide rose higher and higher, Tiger Lily remained ever silent and steadfast. Her captors mistook her silence for nobility, but Tiger Lily felt anything but noble. She closed her eyes in a final attempt to block out the image of her father in pain when he would find her lifeless body.

But her thoughts were suddenly interrupted by the sound of his voice.

"Hand over my daughter!"

Even from afar, Chief Great Little Big Panther's command was strong and forceful. Tiger Lily opened her eyes. Across the bay, the chief and Captain Hook stared at each other, squaring off.

"It's either the old woman doesn't know how to relay a message or foolish chiefs don't listen," Hook sneered.

The chief was about to attack Hook, who stood glaring repugnantly at him, when one of his men called out, "Over there!"

The chief looked to where the young warrior was pointing and locked eyes with his only daughter, bound to a rock in the middle of the lagoon. The tide was nearly covering her head. The chief leaped past Hook and slid down the rocky edge of the grotto, grunting as the sharp rocks pierced his body.

"GET HIM!" Captain Hook ordered the onlooking pirates. Obediently the pirates shimmied down after the chief, duplicating the same painful grunts as they climbed down the jagged rocks.

The chief made it successfully down the ridge and was about to dive into the water when he was suddenly bowled over by one of the pirates who had jumped the rest of the way down. The pirate took the chief down with his weight and with the help of the other pirates, pinned the flailing chief to the ground.

As the chief lay struggling beneath the pirates, the battle ensued between his warriors and the rest of Captain Hook's men. It took five of Captain Hook's pirates to contain the raging chief. Unable to break free, he could only howl in anger as Captain Hook sauntered by, gesturing with his arm for the chief to set eyes on Tiger Lily.

"NO!" he cried.

Peter and his Lost Boys arrived on the island to a raging battle. The Lost Boys wasted no time and joined in, but Peter headed straight for Tiger Lily, hastily manoeuvring past the swarms of desperate pirates attempting to grab him.

Peter's speed and agility allowed him to get to the bottom of the rocks with ease, but Captain Hook stood between him and the water—and Tiger Lily.

"Let her go! It is me you're after!" shouted Peter Pan, brandishing his knife.

Captain Hook drew his sword and smiled.

"You don't know how long I have waited for this moment," snarled the captain. "I am going to make you regret the day you ever left that orphanage!"

Captain Hook lunged his heavy sword at Peter in every direction, but Peter dodged the powerful swipes and danced around to avoid Hook's massive blade, much like the battle years before. Once again, Peter's speed played in his favour—but this time around, there were no ship decks and masts for Peter to hide behind. Hook's smart swordsmanship allowed him to quickly back Peter into the rocks.

Captain Hook raised his sword to Peter's throat. Peter stood frozen against the rocks as the captain slowly ran his hook up Peter's torso, tearing apart his clothes and leaving a gash across his skin. Peter groaned in agonized pain.

This was the event that the pirates had all been waiting for—their captain would finally have his revenge. The battle ceased momentarily and not a sound could be heard as they all looked on.

The chief, however, never broke his concentration. He took advantage of this lapse in judgment by the pirates and broke free from their hold. He reached down into the cuff of his moccasin and pulled out a knife, and while still kneeling, Chief Great Little Big Panther hurled the knife across the water at Captain Hook.

The small blade struck Captain Hook in the middle of his back and lodged itself deep inside. Hook cried out in pain as he fell to his knees, his sword falling out of his hand.

Peter pushed aside the immobilized captain and kicked his sword into the water. Pulling the knife from the captain's back, Peter plunged into the ice-cold water where the tide had just risen above Tiger Lily's head. In one enormous breath, Peter filled his lungs with air and dived down to find her. The chief had already taken to the water from the opposite end of the grotto but was still too far to reach his daughter in time.

Minutes passed, and Peter still had not emerged from below. Chief Great Little Big Panther had gone under several times, coming up empty-handed each time. He looked around in panic and bewilderment. Each failed attempt brought him closer to losing his daughter for good.

Peter burst out of the water with Tiger Lily in his arms. Together he and the chief pulled her listless body onto shore.

Wasting no time, Peter rolled the lifeless princess onto her back and cupped her head in his hands. The petrified chief held her hand as Peter tried to resuscitate her.

"Please, Creator, do not take her!" he prayed as he watched Peter breathe frantically into his daughter's blue lips.

Suddenly Tiger Lily's body responded. She coughed up water and, her eyes springing open, she gasped for air. Chief Great Little Big Panther grabbed her, sobbing, and sat her upright as an exhausted Peter fell to the ground. The chief held his daughter as she cried in his arms and tried to regain her stability.

With Tiger Lily out of danger, Peter's attention was averted across the grotto to the pirates, who were crouched over their captain. There would be no escape for them. The few pirates who survived the attack on shore had already deserted their men and fled in their captain's ship when they saw their leader fall, with the Piccaninny warriors close behind them. There would be nowhere or no way for the others to escape. They were left to die there with their captain.

That evening, the tribe would celebrate Tiger Lily's rescue by honouring Peter with a great feast and ceremonial dancing.

The events of the day were enough to help Tiger Lily temporarily forget her grief over Jerrekai and she found herself smiling and laughing again. She was even so giddy that she allowed herself to be mildly flirtatious with Peter, though he made it quite easy—his adoration for her was obvious. In those moments she was reminded of her youthful beauty and her power to captivate men, even men not of her own land. However, her smile quickly faded. *Beauty was not enough to keep the heart of the man I loved.* She thanked Peter once again for saving her life and announced to the tribe that she was to retire for the night.

As she rose to leave, Peter asked if he could escort her safely home. Tiger Lily hesitated then agreed politely; she couldn't dare risk offending her father by refusing this gesture.

They strode toward her hut in silence, the music and laughter of the party growing fainter with each step. Peter was the first to speak.

"It sure is a pretty night."

"Yes, quite pretty," Tiger Lily answered shortly. She did not want to start a conversation.

They strolled in silence a few more steps before Peter spoke again, "I think you're pretty too."

"Thank you."

Gone were the days when Tiger Lily's heart would beat thunderous booms and her belly would fill with a thousand butterflies at receiving a compliment like that from a man. Tiger Lily knew she could not return his affection and Peter was too great a man to allow him false hope.

"Peter, my journey has already begun, and yours has yet to start." She spoke with more confidence than she realized she had. "I have already loved another and because he still has my heart, I cannot give it to you now."

"I can wait," Peter said.

Tiger Lily stopped walking. "But I cannot guarantee that you would not wait forever."

Peter's head dropped with the weight of rejection. Tiger Lily turned his chin up so that she could look upon his green eyes.

"You are a warrior of the highest calibre and I should be lucky to be by your side." She smiled gently at Peter. "If I could love you today I would, but you, Peter Pan, will remain my true friend for life. That I promise you."

Tiger Lily kissed Peter on the cheek and thanked him one last time. There was nothing more to be said. Peter tipped his hat to bid Tiger Lily farewell and headed back in the direction of the celebration. Tiger Lily, however, did not go inside her hut. Instead, she found herself walking down the same familiar path that she had walked so joyfully only moons before.

At the edge of the clearing Tiger Lily looked out into the distance across the still waters, as though if she looked hard enough, she could see the outline of Jerrekai's boat sailing home along the horizon line. But alas, the one last plea of a broken heart was to no avail; there was no boat and no Jerrekai. Her happiness had gone on without her and nothing behind her could bring her joy. Tiger Lily so longed for Jerrekai and the life that she had planned for them. Now that it was not to be, she no longer knew what was to become of her—and it scared her to even wonder.

CHAPTER 6

The Horizon

Mud oozed up past her ankles as she gasped for breath, terrified that it may be her last. And then like a catapult, Tiger Lily shot up in her bed, her scream escaping in full breath. Father rushed to her side, as he was never too far away.

The dreams had become a common occurrence, so much that Chief Great Little Big Panther barely slept at night. He would sit up by the fire carving pipes and trinkets to keep busy. Some nights he would just sit and stare into the flames, praying for the dreams to cease and his precious Tiger Lily to be returned to the carefree, happy girl she once was.

The dreams were always the same: Tiger Lily was stuck in the middle of a swamp, unable to lift her feet from the mud. Behind her was darkness, angst, fear, and a deep emptiness. Ahead of her, off in the distance, was brightness—beautiful and colourful and glistening, a world yet to be explored. Tiger Lily needed only to free herself from the mud and move forward. But each time she tried to take a step, she could not. Her feet were so firmly planted that she was powerless to move, and when she tried to cry out she realized that she couldn't talk. The panic was instant and she began to fight for air... In that moment she would wake with a jolt, panting to catch her breath.

Two winters had passed since that fateful night she was rescued from Mermaid's Lagoon. Two winters since she watched Jerrekai sail out of her life. Two winters since she last wore her mother's feather...and since she last heard the voice of her grandmother.

After the attack, Grandmother never fully recovered her strength. In her weakened state, Grandmother was left without the use of her voice. Her only way of communicating was with her eyes, her touch, and her smile.

Even when Tiger Lily sat crying at her bedside, apologizing for leaving the hut that night when she was supposed to stay indoors, Grandmother would muster up a smile, and in the final moments before her death, when Tiger Lily attempted to apologize yet again, Grandmother used the last bit of strength she had to lift her tiny wrinkled hand to Tiger Lily's lips to silence her. It was Grandmother's way of telling Tiger Lily that she had forgiven her, but Tiger Lily couldn't forgive herself. She had yet to reveal to her father that it was she who led the pirates to their hut that night. If she had stayed put like her father had instructed her to, the pirates might never have taken her and tied up Grandmother.

Many times Tiger Lily wanted to tell her father that it was her fault, but each time she couldn't find the words. She knew Grandmother had forgiven her, but what if he couldn't? What if he found out that her carelessness and her selfishness had caused Grandmother's death? He was the only family she had left. Tiger Lily just could not take that chance. Instead, Tiger Lily held her secret inside and told no one, not even Nascha, and allowed it to rest heavily on her already broken heart.

She was consumed by her guilt, heartbreak, and loneliness. She could feel it changing her; tears could flow easily now but laughter was difficult. She smiled less and preferred to be alone most days.

The pain of losing Jerrekai was never too far from Tiger Lily's thoughts. Every man she had met, she would compare to the young builder. She could always find something wrong with them. Eventually, and to her relief, the suitors had just stopped trying. But as life went on without love or the prospect of it, Tiger Lily began to grow sad. This was no longer just a sadness of the heart but a sadness of some other making. This change in Tiger Lily caused great conflict and burden on Chief Great Little Big Panther. He blamed himself heavily for taking her away. "Let me travel north," he offered. "I'll bring Jerrekai back."

Chief Great Little Big Panther was desperate to restore his daughter's happiness, but Tiger Lily refused and assured her father that he was not to blame. She knew that bringing Jerrekai back was not the answer, although the thought did intrigue her. If her father would have posed that question in the days after Jerrekai's departure, she very well may have agreed. But too much time had passed since then, enough time that the young newlyweds had probably started a family. This was a reality that Tiger Lily was not ready to face. Instead, she confined herself to a place of what ifs. What if she had never left on that voyage?

Would *they* be married? Would *she* have his children? Would Grandmother still be alive?

In the moons that followed, Tiger Lily's heaviness began to ease and she had begun settling into her role as a young lady in the village. She spent her days alongside Nascha and Nascha's mother learning how to bead, sew, prepare meals, and tan hides.

After whole village feasts that she would help to prepare, she and many other tribespeople would sit around the great fire and listen to tales from warriors and legends of long ago. Some nights, the elders would tell of prophecies and visions, and sometimes they would merely talk of work and orders that needed to be done. But when Peter would return from an adventure, tales by the fire would last well into the night. This ritual had gone on nightly ever since she could remember, but this was the first time that Tiger Lily had joined in.

She could remember Jerrekai engaging in conversations while she waited impatiently for him to be done. She never realized at the time that if she bothered to pay any attention, she might actually enjoy many of the stories and discussions.

Some storytellers had a way about sharing lessons that needed to be learned, others told stories full of humour and folly. She learned quickly that there was never a time where someone did not take away something of value from what was shared each evening. And even though she enjoyed the new role she was taking in the village and all the new knowledge she was acquiring, there were moments when it added heaviness to her heart, for it opened her eyes to how immature and self-involved she really was. She wondered if Jerrekai was right to have left her.

It was becoming expected of the younger members of the tribe to begin sharing some words. This scared Tiger Lily and Nascha, who would quickly pass along the talking stick when it came to their turn. If they could manage, they would always try sit to the west of a young man named Iiwatsu. Iiwatsu was a young knowledge seeker. He was the kind of man that would grow up to one day become a wisdom keeper. He was also so long-winded in his stories and questions that the others seemed happy to speed things along afterward.

One evening after the fire, Iiwatsu approached Tiger Lily and Nascha as they helped tidy the grounds.

"Hello Nascha," said Iiwatsu in a kind and pleasing manner.

Nascha blushed and greeted him back, "Hello Iiwatsu, I enjoyed your topic about breeding moose and caribou so that our men no longer need to hunt. I know that the elders weren't too happy, but someday they will see that times are changing."

"Yes, thank you Nascha, I'm happy that you agree."

Iiwatsu was several years older than Tiger Lily and Nascha. Tiger Lily could recall him near the age that she was now, sitting among the elders listening and being mentored, while a young Tiger Lily got into mischief banging her father's drum or trying to pry his knife out of his moccasin. Even though Iiwatsu himself was young at the time, his attention never wandered the way Tiger Lily's did. Even now, Tiger Lily often found her mind trailing off or her attention easily distracted during stories and lessons.

Iiwatsu was not at all tall and not very slender. He had mid-length, thick black hair that he often left untied. And his eyes were quite small in comparison to his large nose and round, bulbous cheeks. However, Tiger Lily did find that he had a rather pleasing smile, and unlike other men, his presence did not intimidate nor unnerve her, as he was quite polite and proper.

"Nascha," Iiwatsu continued, "I was hoping that I could have a word alone with Tiger Lily if you don't mind."

"Oh," said Nascha, clearly taken by surprise.

Tiger Lily waved frantically behind Iiwatsu's back as she mouthed the word "NO" to Nascha. But before Nascha could answer, Iiwatsu turned to face Tiger Lily.

Tiger Lily scanned her surroundings for an excuse, but when she looked past Iiwatsu she could see her father watching them from a distance. Fearful to disappoint him yet again, Tiger Lily agreed.

"Yes, I will accompany you for a walk," she replied sullenly.

As they walked away from the village, Tiger Lily took one last glance over her shoulder at her father, who stood smiling and watching as the pair strolled away.

In the days that followed, the evening outings with Iiwatsu became a regular occurrence. He led their conversations with philosophical ideals and ponderings about the meaning of life and creation. Tiger Lily would just walk and listen. Although she was fond of Iiwatsu and found him interesting, she did not feel an attraction to him in the way she did with Jerrekai, and when he would talk, her mind would often trail off into a comparison of the two.

Jerrekai liked to carve musical instruments and hunting utensils, where Iiwatsu liked to talk about the different uses for musical instruments and hunting utensils. Jerrekai had an adventurous spirit, where Iiwatsu was grounded and safe. Iiwatsu sat in his hut and stared at a fire for hours analyzing the flames, where Jerrekai spent hours outdoors resurrecting homes in the hot sun. The only thing the two had in common was that they were both kind in spirit and respectful to everyone who crossed their paths. Tiger Lily admired that quality greatly. It was also a quality that Walking Bear did not possess in her brief courtship with him. Had he even an ounce of the genuineness and sensitivity of either Jerrekai or Iiwatsu, she could have learned to love him, and maybe she would have never run into the woods that day and she would have never fallen in love with Jerrekai. Her heart would never have been broken and she would not be caught in between her longing for what she could never have and resistance to what was in front of her.

So many what ifs still plagued Tiger Lily's mind. She was grateful that Iiwatsu was not interested in her life story, for she would surely not be able to keep the tears from welling up in her eyes if she were to speak aloud of Jerrekai. However, the feelings that Tiger Lily still had for Jerrekai did not deter her from spending time with Iiwatsu, for as much as he liked to talk, he did not profess matters of the heart, and though she sensed Iiwatsu was fond of her, Tiger Lily did not worry that romantic inclinations would arise unexpectedly. She was grateful for his company and to have someone to help pass the days.

Still, when the sun left the sky, Tiger Lily would often sneak back out to the clearing and listen in solidarity to the waves rush up against the rocks. The sound would always take her back to the night she found Jerrekai sitting in the rain.

One afternoon as Tiger Lily sat in her hut weaving a basket for berry picking, Father came in grinning. A smile quickly spread across her face as well. She hadn't seen him this happy in a long time—whatever it was that elated him this much, she was eager to hear about. Tiger Lily put down her project and waited intently to hear what Father had to say.

"Tiger Lily, I have just come from the meeting hut where, in front of the grand council of elders, Iiwatsu has just asked me for your hand."

Tiger Lily gasped. Immediately her heart sank—she did not want to marry Iiwatsu; she did not want to marry at all. Her heart belonged to Jerrekai. If she couldn't have him, she didn't want anyone. She would remain alone to the end of her days.

There was a long silence as father and daughter stared at each other. Tiger Lily's smile had disappeared completely.

"Well?" said Father. "Are you going to say anything?" His smile was also gone.

"Sorry Father, I was just taken by surprise," Tiger Lily answered truthfully. "I did not know that Iiwatsu felt this way about me."

"As is the way it should be," the chief piped up confidently. "A young lady should not be running about looking for her own husband."

Tiger Lily's head dropped. She couldn't bring herself to look him in the eyes as he continued.

"This is the way it has always been done. And this is the way it should have been done." Chief Great Little Big Panther's voice was getting louder and louder. "I don't know what that boy said or did to you that made you believe you were in love. But if he had any sense in his head, he would have come to me like a man instead of filling your head with crazy ideas!"

"Father, he wasn't…"

"SILENCE!" the chief boomed.

Chief Great Little Big Panther walked over to Tiger Lily and knelt beside her.

"Iiwatsu may not be a great warrior, but he will take good care of you. He gave me his word."

Tiger Lily looked into her father's loving eyes. He too had been hanging on to a dream just as she had been.

"I will consider his request," Tiger Lily said. "Can I tell you my answer in the morning?"

"Yes," the chief agreed.

Tiger Lily had successfully managed to avoid her father and Iiwatsu all the next day. As she stood at the edge of the escarpment staring down at the ferocity of the waves crashing up against the rocks, Tiger Lily wondered if they were strong enough to break bones, or even to take a life.

"Why do you still come here?"

This question pierced through Tiger Lily's ears like a spear. She spun around to see a stern-faced Nascha standing behind her.

"What?"

"This spot, Tiger Lily! Why do you still come here?" Nascha's eyes demanded an answer, but Tiger Lily turned away. "What kind of torture do you have planned for yourself, Tiger Lily? Why do you continue to punish yourself? You didn't do anything wrong!"

Nascha's words elicited a shame that Tiger Lily did not feel strong enough to face.

"I know about Iiwatsu. He has asked for your hand, but you have yet to accept. What is it you are waiting for, Tiger Lily? You know Jerrekai is not coming back. Why can't you just move on?"

This was the first time that her friend had ever been so forceful with Tiger Lily.

"You don't understand," said Tiger Lily.

"You're right. I don't understand!" yelled Nascha. "You've had four men in love with you, Tiger Lily, and numerous others vying for your hand, and I've had none! So yes, I don't understand!"

Tiger Lily looked up to see that her friend had tears in her eyes.

"I would love for someone as kind as Iiwatsu to want to marry me, or someone as adventurous as Peter Pan to even take an interest in me. But not you, Tiger Lily!"

Nascha scolded. "You are throwing away a chance at love with both hands."

My self-absorbed ways have prevented me from taking into consideration anyone's feelings but my own. Tiger Lily had never asked Nascha how she felt or if she was even looking for love, but she was. She wanted love just as much as Tiger Lily did.

"You're right, Nascha," Tiger Lily admitted. "I do need to move forward, and I am sorry if I was not a good friend."

"It's all right," said Nascha, offering her friend an empathetic smile. "No one is perfect."

Tiger Lily walked to the edge of the cliff and stared out into the sea. Without turning her gaze from the water, she finally spoke. "What if I told you I have been lying to myself all this time?" said Tiger Lily, more so to herself than to her friend. "I knew that there would have been no way I could have made Jerrekai stay. I could not change what the Creator had planned." Tiger Lily paused as if to dig deeper into herself. "I also knew that there was no way that he could have ever loved me the way he loved her."

In the silence, she allowed the words to leave her mouth and travel back into her own ears.

"He didn't feel worthy of me," Tiger Lily confessed, wiping a tear from her cheek. "There would have never been a balance, I know this now. He would have forever walked in my shadow…and how could anyone be happy in the dark?" Tiger Lily looked around at her familiar surroundings. "I was selfish. I would have kept him in the dark, just so I could be happy, and I would have been happy, because I am selfish."

"You are not selfish."

"Yes I am!" Tiger Lily snapped. "Look at what I have done to my poor father. He is weakened because of me! Look what I have done to our village. They have gone on without a leader because their leader is too preoccupied with his selfish daughter! And my poor grandmother, she died because of me."

"No she didn't, it wasn't—"

"YES SHE DID!" Tiger Lily spun around so that she was standing face to face with Nascha. "I was supposed to stay inside that night. But I didn't listen. I was too busy feeling sorry for myself, and then they came. They followed me back to my hut. I never told anyone this. It is my fault she is dead! It is my fault that my father's men died that day in Mermaid's Lagoon! And yet here I am still crying over Jerrekai!"

The pair stood in silence for a few minutes. Nascha was the first to speak.

"Tiger Lily, if the pirates were coming for you, they would have found you. Maybe you made it just a bit easier. But I'd like to tell you what my own grandmother used to tell me. She said that everything in this life happens for a reason. Creator has many plans for our lives and sets before us many trials so that we may learn quickly all that we need in order for us to carry out our destiny. Your grandmother's death was in his plan, just as it was in his plan for you to be captured, for Jerrekai to leave, and for Walking Bear to fall. It is what you take forward with you that matters." Nascha held Tiger Lily's hands. "Many hardships have fallen on you, my dear friend, more so than I would ever be able to handle. Maybe that just means that Creator has big plans for you and you need to be prepared."

Tiger Lily took in the words of her friend. She knew that the wisdom of the grandmothers was not to be ignored. Without her own grandmother to share her stories, Tiger Lily was grateful to have Nascha share the wisdom she truly needed at this time.

"Thank you, Nascha," said Tiger Lily through her sobs.

Nascha embraced her friend and the pair cried in each other's arms as the wind carried their calls into the sky. When they had cried all they could cry, Tiger Lily got up and helped her friend to her feet.

"I know what I need to do first… Father deserves to know the truth, even if it tears us apart. I feel too removed from him when there are lies between us."

"Your father loves you and he will forgive you," Nascha assured.

"I will also tell him that I will accept Iiwatsu."

"Tiger Lily," Nascha interrupted, "you do not need to enter into anything you are not ready for. I didn't mean to pressure you."

"No, Nascha, you were right," Tiger Lily said. "I need to move on. For the first time since Jerrekai left, I feel ready to take back my life and carve out my future. You helped me to see that." Tiger Lily looked all around. "This place has been home to much happiness for me, but also to so much pain," she declared. "I have been punishing myself by hanging on, but I will leave it here today and I won't come back to this place."

When those words left her lips, Tiger Lily knew that she was no longer speaking only about the clearing. She was speaking about the place of sadness she brought her heart to every time she relived memories of the past.

With Nascha by her side, Tiger Lily made the decision to free herself from the mud. She would let go of the past and choose the path not taken. It was time to look for new horizons and to paint a new picture for her life.

The pair walked back to the village hand-in-hand, and for once in a very long time, Tiger Lily felt hopeful that the new moons would once again bring happiness into her heart. Little did she know that what the Creator had in store for her was beyond anything she could have ever imagined for herself.

Part Two

CHAPTER 7

They Came Bearing Gifts

The deep, crisp air of spring engulfed Tiger Lily's lungs as she emerged from her hut to greet the sunrise. She wanted to meet this day in solitude and give her thanks to the Creator alone before Iiwatsu woke.

Privacy was hard to manage these days. Tiger Lily was always surrounded by people trying to make her comfortable or give her words of advice and wanting to handle her protruding belly. She relished in the quietness of her mornings when she would have the world to herself and she could talk openly to her unborn baby.

Life was serene. Iiwatsu was a very good husband; he was loyal, kind, and attentive, especially when Tiger Lily was getting ready to welcome their child. And even though Iiwatsu and her father were so different, Tiger Lily saw in him the qualities of her father that she loved so dearly.

To the outside world, they both painted an elaborate picture of what their role was supposed to be. Father was a strong and fierce leader, while Iiwatsu was a seeker of knowledge—a philosopher. But in the presence of Tiger

Lily, both men allowed themselves to be vulnerable and unknowing, sometimes allowing her to see that they didn't have all the answers, only faith that they were doing right. Tiger Lily admired this quality in them both so much, so she didn't mind that Iiwatsu and her father were both at her side nearly every minute of every day in the days leading up to the impending arrival of her little one. Tiger Lily was grateful for it all. She could also see how happy it made everyone around to know that soon Chief Great Little Big Panther would have reason to celebrate.

It was known that Chief Great Little Big Panther had suffered greatly in his time. After the tragic loss of his wife and son, he masked the pain of what was beyond his control by controlling everything else around him. He quickly secured the best army of warriors, the most land, the grandest huts, ships, and weapons, and the largest vessel of wealth.

But all the control in the world could not grant him control over his daughter's strong and steadfast heart. Tiger Lily emulated her father's strength in so many ways that it was her strength that had weakened him the most. But that was behind them now; the chief was happy again and his happiness swelled over onto the people and they all felt the call to rejoice.

As Tiger Lily stepped out of the hut that early spring morning, she knew that today would be the day, for it wasn't the morning air that woke her up, it was the dull pain in her back that seemed to grow ever so slightly throughout the night, finally making its way down to settle in the small of her back.

Tiger Lily walked down to the water and, with much struggle, knelt to peer over. She stared expressionless at the reflection of the girl with the braids. She wanted to capture the last moment of youth and innocence before it would be gone forever. Tiger Lily did not feel sad, nor did she long for this moment to be delayed, but she did feel a sense of loss to have to say goodbye to the carefree child she was leaving behind.

With both hands raised to the sky, Tiger Lily gave her thanks to the Creator for this day, for her husband, her father, her friend Nascha, and her new baby. She called on the spirit of her mother and grandmother for guidance, strength, and protection. She also asked them to watch over Father, as she felt more nervous for him than she did for herself. Tiger Lily knew that the birth of one's first child was a long process that sometimes lasted over days. She knew the fear and anticipation he would be going through having the last experience with childbirth end so sorrowfully. Tiger Lily asked for one last prayer of safety. She could not bear the thought of her father's broken heart.

At the suggestion of the mothers in the village, Tiger Lily was to walk all day. Even after supper when the nightly ritual was to sit and rest by the fire and listen to stories, Tiger Lily was to keep moving. The discomfort was great and her urge to lie down was constant, but she did as she was told and kept moving. Tiger Lily was determined to battle against her own selfish inclinations and heeded the advice of her elders. She did not want her child to be born into this world amid weakness and fear. If she had any control over the situation, she would fight these feelings with every ounce of courage and bravery she could muster.

She and Nascha walked the outskirts of the village, taking care not to stray too far, but just far enough that the sounds of the busyness would not disturb their own discussions. They talked about how if her child were a boy, he would be named after her father, and if it were a girl, Red Seneca after her mother. They spoke of how Iiwatsu had recently approached her father about having a hut resurrected on a hilltop apart from the village. At first he vehemently disagreed, but when Iiwatsu explained that Tiger Lily wanted privacy as her small child was growing, Father agreed.

It was no secret that Tiger Lily's life was an open book. From the moment she was betrothed to Walking Bear and through all the stages of her heartbreak and healing from Jerrekai, Tiger Lily's personal life had always been on display. Now with the new baby coming, and the preparation for the potlatch—a large-scale feast and ceremony to celebrate momentous occasions—it had grown much worse.

In the wee hours of the morning, Nascha emerged from the hut to make an announcement to the small crowd of villagers who had stayed to fellowship with the chief and Iiwastu as they waited patiently, and not without nervousness, outside the birthing hut.

Peter Pan and his Lost Boys were also in attendance. They had sailed home from one of their adventures to show their unwavering support to their chief.

"It's a boy!" Nascha exclaimed, throwing her hands wildly into their air.

The crowd erupted in cheers as the each took turns patting the shoulders of the chief and Iiwatsu.

Tiger Lily decided on the name Peter Iiwatsu Little Panther, though he would lovingly be referred to as Pip. Even before his birth, Pip had begun to restore the love and happiness back into Tiger Lily's life. Her heart swelled with joy at the sight of her son so perfect and pure. She had no idea that one tiny creature could have so much power, and it was in those little first of his little life that Tiger Lily would watch as Pip grew the love between herself and Iiwatsu. Their hearts overflowed with love for him and that love spilled over onto each other.

Iiwatsu doted on Tiger Lily now more than ever before, rubbing her back as she fed Pip in the middle of the night and brushing her hair in the morning when she woke, tired from long nights. Tiger Lily watched as Iiwatsu went about his day and his duties with as little sleep as she had and without any complaints. Life was good. Iiwatsu and Tiger Lily marvelled at each new day watching him grow together.

The day had finally come for the three-day potlach celebration that was heralded as the largest of the west coast. Heads of tribes from all the surrounding nations and beyond had begun ascending on the shores of the Piccaninny waters. They came in droves on canoes, ships, horseback, and foot, dressed in their best regalia and bearing gifts for the baby and gifts honouring the chief and his tribe. In return, they would leave with gifts reflecting the gratitude and wealth of the host tribe. A magnificent array of colours glistened in the sunlight as beautifully painted horses carrying elaborately dressed men and women gathered to greet one another.

In the centre of it all was Chief Great Little Big Panther, and beside him, Peter Pan. Though Tiger Lily felt honoured by the grand celebration, it was her wish to be as far away from the crowds and commotion as she could. She welcomed the opportunity to settle into the background and occasionally make her way into the feasting grounds to help out and sample the food.

The food prepared for the three days was enough to feed her entire tribe for a year. Their village had harvested and gathered tirelessly all season. During the feast preparation, it was revealed that the women in the tribe had begun gathering seeds the day after it was announced that Tiger Lily would be married, as surely a baby would be not far along after. *My villagers care so deeply for their chief that they would go to these lengths to celebrate him.* Tiger Lily could not express the gratitude she felt. The only way she felt that she could repay them was by vowing to raise her son to be as noble as her father so that when he grew to be a man, he would lead with the same loyalty and devotion as he did. She was, after all, raising the next chief.

For the next three days and nights, political leaders and political enemies put their differences aside and enjoyed the atmosphere of feasting, dancing, performances, and gift giving in the great hall, which had been resurrected for this sole purpose.

It was a grand celebration, each day more lavish and magnificent than the day previous. But on the last day, an unsettling fear began to arise. For the first time, Peter had been absent from her father's side, and as the dancing continued into the afternoon, he nor any of the Lost Boys had not made their appearance. She couldn't imagine what could be so important that it would keep him away all day.

Finally, late that afternoon, Tiger Lily saw one of the Lost Boys rushing toward the chief. Chief Great Little Big Panther's attention was drawn immediately to the young man.

The sound of the drums and the singing made it impossible for Tiger Lily to hear anything that was said, but as soon as the chief got up to leave the great hall without a word to anyone, instinctively she knew something was wrong.

Tiger Lily painted a smile on her face and handed the baby off to Iiwatsu before following her father. But she was not quick enough—her father and the Lost Boy were nowhere in sight.

Some time had passed when the chief finally returned. Tiger Lily scanned the hall and still she did not see Peter or a single Lost Boy.

What is going on? The answer would have to wait; it was the end of the potlatch and time to say goodbye.

Tiger Lily, Pip, and Iiwatsu took their place beside her father and one by one said their farewells and thanked their guests. But Tiger Lily couldn't help but to notice her father's somewhat distracted demeanour.

When the last of the guests exited the great hall, Tiger Lily was finally able to probe her father with questions. "Father, what is going on? Where are Peter and the Lost Boys?"

"Oh, it's nothing for you to worry about," he answered, clearly avoiding eye contact. "Go on and get little Pip into bed. I have to get going, I still have a lot to do."

The chief tried exiting, but Tiger Lily was insistent on getting an answer. "Father, please," she begged. "I need to know what's going on. I've seen this look before and I'm afraid."

Tiger Lily had to fight back the tears she felt welling up. She could not escape this mounting sense of fear that had only intensified as the night wore on.

The chief looked into his daughter's glassy eyes. "Peter and his Lost Boys noticed ships circling the waters today," he finally confessed. "He figures they may have been pirate ships."

Tiger Lily cupped her mouth to contain her gasp.

"They have gone out to search the waters and to keep the passageways clear as people get ready to head home."

"Pirates?" she repeated. "What would pirates be doing here? Hook is dead. What could they want?"

"We don't know for certain, so I didn't want to alarm you or anyone else. We just want to be on the safe side. But don't worry, I will not let anything happen to you or little Pip."

But for the first time in a very long time, Tiger Lily felt fearful of the pirates. She now had little Pip to protect and she could not let anything happen to him—he was her life.

By first light, the guests had begun their journeys home and the Piccaninny villagers were already busy clearing and cleaning and sifting through the gifts that had amassed over the three days.

The men had begun taking down the tipis and clearing away debris. Women were busy airing out the blankets, organizing the pots and precious metals, fabrics and leathers, meat, jewellery, clothing, and masks. Although the celebration was over, there was still so much to be done and no one in the village was without a job to do.

From the feast house where Tiger Lily was helping prepare meals for the hardworking villagers, she saw that Peter and his Lost Boys had returned. She put down her utensils and hurried after them, but they retreated into the meeting hut of the grand council before she could catch up.

The grand council consisted of the oldest living members of the tribe along with knowledge keepers, healers, the highest-ranking warriors, the chief, and Peter. But Tiger Lily was not about to be left out. She took a deep breath and burst through the door, prompting everyone to turn and stare at her in complete silence.

"Go on," she urged. "I am not leaving, so you may as well continue."

All eyes moved to Chief Great Little Big Panther, who granted her stay by gesturing her to sit. "It's all right," he declared. "She knows what is going on."

The group settled into their places to await the news they had all been summoned for.

"It was a pirate ship that Peter had seen," the chief reported, to a collective gasp. "We do not know who is captaining the ship," he continued. "But we were able to chase them far off. They won't be coming back anytime soon."

Tiger Lily fought to steady her breathing and mask the fear that was causing her heart to palpitate.

"Peter has decided to postpone his trip east and stay on until winter so that he can patrol the waters in case they try to come back," announced the chief.

The grand council nodded toward Peter in appreciation.

"Though they would be crazy to try attack us," the chief said, his voice becoming raised in fury. "We outnumber them greatly and even our weapons alone that we have collected these last three days have put us in such a great position of power, no man can touch us."

Chief Great Big Little Panther's words were strong and full of conviction. He believed what he said and so did Peter and the others. In that moment, Tiger Lily's own fears were eased and she felt safe again from any direct threat of pirates. Her father was right; they were in an untouchable position—but how wrong they all were.

CHAPTER 8

In the Mist

The work resumed for the Piccaninny Tribe. The early-morning air was filled with chatter as each tribe member was up with the sun, working tirelessly to restore their village after having accommodated hundreds of guests. Although exhausted, the tribe was fuelled by the energy and excitement of the last three days. The mood in the village was happy and grateful as children ran about while adults were hard at work. The village was beginning to resemble what it had been before the droves of people came through.

Near the end of the work, it seemed as though the fatigue had begun to catch up with some. A few of the women began to take ill, and two elderly women became so sick that they were bedridden with fever.

Chief Great Little Big Panther spread the word that everyone must take a day of rest. The majority of the work had been done, and their health was more important. The preparation and execution of the potlatch had consumed so much time and energy from everyone that the chief did not want anyone getting sick on this account.

Yet it had now been nearly ten days since the potlatch had ended and the two elderly women who had taken ill saw their health declining rapidly. Both women began to develop sores on their bodies from the high fever. Five other women and two children had also taken ill with fever and had to be confined to bed rest. This illness was clearly not the result of exhaustion and fatigue.

The sickness began to make its way quickly through the village. With each day that passed, more and more elderly men and women and some children began to show signs of the same sickness. After the twelfth day, the first elderly woman lost her life, and the next day, two more women. An emergency meeting of the grand council was called.

Tiger Lily watched as the members filed one by one into the hut. Though she had been permitted to stay during the last meeting, she was not at liberty to invite herself to any further meetings. She would have to wait to hear the news just like everyone else.

But before the chief went into the hut, he turned back in the direction of Tiger Lily and Iiwatsu. "Iiwatsu, come." He motioned for Iiwatsu to join him. "Tiger Lily," he said.

"Yes, Father?"

"Take little Pip home and wait there."

"Yes, Father."

Tiger Lily had half-hoped for an invitation as well, but even though she did not get it, she was grateful that Iiwatsu had. After all, her motives were strictly informational, whereas Iiwatsu would provide service.

When the meeting was over, Chief Great Little Big Panther made no haste in leading the way for Iiwatsu back to the hut where Tiger Lily and Pip sat awaiting the news of the meeting.

"Tiger Lily!" the chief boomed as he burst through the door. "Is Pip showing any signs of the sores? Have you been near the healing lodge?"

"No Father, I have been helping in the feast hall with the cooking."

"I don't want you two leaving this hut."

"What about the cooking?"

"I will not repeat myself and I will not be disobeyed!" the chief commanded.

"Okay, Father, we won't leave," Tiger Lily promised.

"Iiwatsu, until we know what this illness is, you cannot hold your son or wife." This was the chief's last order before he walked away.

"Iiwatsu, what is happening?" asked a bewildered Tiger Lily.

"People are dying, Tiger Lily, and it is not just in our village. Many of the people that left here have not made it home. At this time, it is not known how many are sick. The men have already left to go bring back the numbers."

Tiger Lily gasped. Some of the tribespeople who had attended the potlatch had also developed the same illness, and many died before they made it back to their shores.

"The five elderly women who were showing signs of illness are not responding to any medicines," Iiwatsu said. The grand council came to a swift decision that all people showing signs of illness must be quarantined in the great hall, the same hall where only days before had been home to laughter and celebration. They would be cared for by the healthy young women with no children. The warriors were divided into groups to visit the neighbouring tribes to learn more of this illness and seek the knowledge of a proper treatment. "Your father is right, Tiger Lily," Iiwatsu finished. "It is not safe for you and Pip out there. I pray this will pass quickly, but until then I must keep my distance from you and Pip until we know what this is. We can't take any chances."

Tiger Lily looked over at her infant son, who lay sleeping, so peaceful and innocent. She could not bear to lose him.

The illness swept rapidly throughout the village. Each day, the number of people who grew ill multiplied. Tiger Lily could do nothing but pace in her hut waiting for some sort of news from the grand council. Iiwatsu had stopped coming home altogether when some members of the grand council had taken ill. He and Chief Great Little Big Panther checked in daily with Tiger Lily and baby Pip by knocking on the side of the wall. They refused to even allow her to open a window and converse, so exchanges would have to be through the thickness of her enclosure.

Finally, the men had begun arriving back to the village with news of the other tribes brought to the grand council.

"Chief Great Little Big Panther," began White Buffalo, a seasoned warrior. "The tribes of the most westerly shores were hit the hardest with death and disease. The Qahatika, Chimariko, the Skokomish have all been devastated."

As the day went on, more and more warriors had begun taking their turns entering the council to report their findings.

"Our friend, Chief Strong Arm of Tsetsaut, has also lost his life," reported a young warrior. "This I saw with my own eyes. There is death everywhere. They are calling it the pox."

There was a moment of silence among the grand council while everyone in the room processed the news. Chief Strong Arm was second to Chief Great Little Big Panther as the most feared, strong, and robust chief among all of the neighbouring tribes. This was a great loss, but also instilled an even greater fear. Chief Strong Arm was not elderly, nor weak. If this illness could take him down, there was fear for them all.

The grand council directed that all unaffected women and children must be removed from the village. One by one the healers visited each hut draped in thick clothing, covering all but their eyes. Each member of the family was directed to step out of the hut and reveal their tongue, back, and belly. If they appeared to be in good health, they were given a swatch of leather with a blue marking for each member that was cleared. If any sores on the body or tongue were noticed, the healers presented them with a leather swatch with a red marking. This meant that they would need to make their way to the great hall to be quarantined.

When the healers called into the hut of Tiger Lily and Pip, Iiwatsu and Chief Great Little Big Panther stood nearby to watch in earnest as the two were inspected. When two pieces of blue leather were handed over to Tiger

Lily, she turned in the direction of her father. She could see the ache in his glassy eyes, but he said nothing as she was directed to take only what she needed for the baby and go down to the river.

Tiger Lily left her father's gaze and turned her attention to Iiwatsu. He called out to her, "We are all right!"

Tiger Lily burst into tears as she made her way down the trail to the river, falling in line with the other families. Tears streamed down her face again as she scanned the shoreline of people who were gathered to wait. The number of women and children was much smaller than what she knew resided in their tribe. Her heart broke for all the people who could not join them. But mostly the tears fell for her friend Nascha, who had to stay behind and care for the ill.

It was time to leave. The small group of people boarded Peter's ship and sailed away from their home in silence. The cool wind began to usher people down into the cabin, but Tiger Lily did not join them. She was not yet ready to say goodbye to her home.

Tiger Lily prayed to the Creator for Nascha's safety, for her father, for Iiwatsu, for herself and little Pip, for all the people suffering, and for all the people whose lives were being risked for others. She prayed for Peter and the Lost Boys and their generous hearts. Tiger Lily prayed and prayed and was still praying as the last rays of the sun lowered into the water and they reached the dusky shores of Neverland.

As true as all the tales that were told, Neverland was completely hidden from the naked eye. In a single file line, Tiger Lily and the others followed Peter along the path to the waterfalls and then into the dense forest. They walked in what seemed to be a circular motion, though Tiger Lily could not tell in the dark, until they came to stop in front of a large tree that she was sure they passed some time before. Peter knelt before the tree, pressing both palms against the base of the trunk. No sooner had he touched the tree than it began to move. A large doorway opened, revealing the hollowed-out area inside.

In the dark, Peter led the procession down a makeshift stairway to their underground hideaway. Tiger Lily stumbled forward blindly; the only way to know where she was going was to trust her footing and stay close to the person in front of her. She was never one to be afraid of the dark, but the uncertainty and unfamiliarity of this whole situation unnerved her to her core. *I trust Peter and know he'll keep us safe.*

When they finally reached their underground destination, Peter lit a small lamp. The flame immediately caught another lamp and then another and another, and like magic, the dark space was illuminated with hundreds of tiny flickering lights in every direction. Sounds of awe and fascination broke the silence of the villagers. Children began to giggle and cheer with delight at what their eyes were beholding, Tiger Lily included.

"Oh my, Peter!" she gasped. "It's beautiful."

"Welcome to Neverland," Peter said as he motioned everyone forward.

With baby Pip at her side, Tiger Lily made her way into what looked like a courtyard, a large space filled with ferns and wild flowers and stone trails that led to benches. Ornaments and statues filled the large space, obviously collected from Peter and the Lost Boys' many voyages.

On one side of the courtyard, a large, endless wall was lined with doorways; above each doorway were an even number of windows, indicative of another level, possibly living quarters. On the other side of the courtyard was a large feasting hall where Tiger Lily could see that some of the Lost Boys were already inside preparing a meal for their guests. In the other rooms were areas for woodworking, metal working, reading, cleaning, and even sewing. The way Peter and the Lost Boys had crafted their home was like nothing any of them had ever seen. *It's from another world.*

The mere presence of it all made Tiger Lily look at Peter and his Lost Boys in a new light. They were not just a bunch of young boys living in the trees and taking off on adventures—they were young men who had built themselves a home and who were now giving their beds over to her and her tribe. Tiger Lily felt a lump growing in her throat.

Peter brought news daily to the camp. It seemed that he and his Lost Boys were the only ones who had built up immunity to this strange disease. However, taking no risks, Peter would sail only as far as the shores of the Piccaninny village. Usually Iiwatsu or the chief himself would sail out to meet him and convey messages, bring back supplies and food that the women had prepared, and take any tribespeople who fell ill, which were few. A number of the Lost Boys remained in the village helping in any way they could.

It had been one full moon cycle since the potlatch. Nearly all of the elderly, the weak, and the children who had become sick had died. A few remained very critically ill, but their conditions were not improving, and now some of the young and robust had begun to take ill, as exhaustion from working around the clock had begun to take its toll on their overall health.

Word spread throughout the land that the Piccaninny Tribe and many other tribes of the west and some in the east had been devastated by the pox. The search was on to find the source.

When Peter arrived back from his evening excursion, Tiger Lily waited in the courtyard near the entrance of Neverland as always, to be the first to receive word on her father and Iiwatsu. On this night, Peter did not return her smile and Tiger Lily felt her heartbeat begin to quicken.

"What news do you have from home? How is Father holding up?"

"The chief is well," assured Peter. "He wanted me to relay the message to you that he and his men have gone south in search of answers. He expects to be gone for several days and tells you not to worry."

"And word of Iiwatsu?"

"Iiwatsu is still working tirelessly harvesting medicines. But he does fear that with the season change nearing, he will run out soon."

"Thank you, Peter, for sending me news of my loved ones."

Peter reached out for Tiger Lily's hand, still not returning her smile. "Tiger Lily, Iiwatsu has sent other news for you."

Tiger Lily noticed the seriousness of his look and pulled her hand back. "What is it? If he is well and Father is well, what news might concern me?"

"Tiger Lily…" he started. "Nascha has taken ill."

"Nascha?" Tiger Lily said in disbelief. "But she's young and healthy!"

"I know," said Peter. "That's why he did not want to alarm you earlier. It was hoped that she would get better, but she has taken a turn for the worse."

Tiger Lily took in a shaky breath, stunned. Her dear friend was sick and all this time she had not known! Tiger Lily didn't know whether to run or cry, but there was nowhere for her to go and little Pip was by her side. *What am I to do?*

"Why didn't you tell me earlier?"

"There was nothing you could have done."

"But there is something I could have done!" Tiger Lily snapped. "I could have told her that she was not alone! And that we love her, me and little Pip!"

"She knows, Tiger Lily," said Peter, trying to reassure her.

"How would you know?"

"Because Iiwatsu sat with her each day and comforted her and listened to her."

Tiger Lily's eyes welled up with tears. At that moment she realized just how serious it had all become. In the beauty and comfort of Neverland, she could almost disassociate from the severity of what was really happening just over the water. She burst into sobs and collapsed into Peter's arms.

Tiger Lily did not sleep much that night. She sat by the light of the fire trying to decide on the most meaningful and prominent words that she could say to her friend. For hours, the only words she had scribbled down on the paper Peter had given her were: *I love you*. What could she say to her friend if she were to hear her words for the last time? As much as her heart wanted to believe that Nascha would be fine, her mind forced her to be strong and face the reality that death may find her friend as it did so many others in the tribe.

In the soft light of the last flickering candle, Tiger Lily penned a letter to her friend.

> *My Dearest Nascha,*
>
> *I love you. The sister I never had, you easily became. From the days of chasing butterflies and running from bees, you were my partner in life. My heart wants you to fight, to stay with me and Pip. The selfish girl that you know I am wants you to come back to me. But I know that I am not so selfish in this*

> *request because I know you want to come back to us too. I know you love us with all of your heart. I feel it now as I write this letter. I feel your love so fully that it comforts me in this great time of loneliness. And, my dear Nascha, I know that you feel my great love for you and the love that little Pip has for you. So if you are tired and have to go, I want you to know that your love surrounds us. I will carry you with me all the days ahead until we are reunited again on this earth or in the skies.*
>
> *Your loving sister,*
> *Tiger Lily and baby Pip.*

Peter had agreed to set sail early in the morning to deliver Tiger Lily's letter, and true to his word, there he was waiting in the courtyard. Tiger Lily handed him the tear-stained letter and one last request.

"Peter," she began solemnly. "If Nascha should die, ask Iiwatsu to retrieve the quilled dress I wore when we married. I want her to wear it when her body returns to the earth."

"I will," promised Peter. He gave Tiger Lily a much-needed embrace and was gone.

Tiger Lily paced the day away waiting for news. But when night fell and Peter was still not back, her anticipation was replaced with worry. It wasn't until the next evening that Peter finally emerged in the courtyard wearing the same solemn look as the last time he returned. A wave of panic set in again and Tiger Lily wished she were still waiting.

"Tiger Lily, please sit," said Peter, motioning her to the bench.

Tiger Lily did as she was told and Peter took the seat next to her.

"I'm sorry Tiger Lily, but Nascha did not make it." Tiger Lily buried her face into Peter's chest, sobs wracking her body. "But before she died, I read her your letter."

Tiger Lily had prayed all night and all day that her friend would pull through. *I never fully allowed myself to believe that I might actually lose Nascha.* She didn't want to imagine a world where she would have to go through life without her. Nascha was to find love and have children, and they would grow old together—and now none of it would ever come to be. How horrible and unforgiving this disease was.

"Tiger Lily," Peter said, still holding her. "I have more news to tell you."

"No, I don't want to hear any more about this devastation..."

"Tiger Lily," he interrupted. He placed his hands on her shoulders and prompted her to look up. "Iiwatsu died this morning."

A shrill ringing filled her ears, and the ground fell away. Tiger Lily looked at Peter in shock. "What?"

"I'm so sorry, Tiger Lily. I didn't know he was sick. No one knew. He hid it from everybody, and there wasn't any way to tell, everyone is so heavily covered."

Tiger Lily stared blankly at Peter, bewildered. *This is a dream,* she thought numbly.

"He was a brave man, Tiger Lily, braver than any warrior," Peter declared. "I went to your hut and I retrieved your dress and Iiwatsu's painted vest… We burned their bodies today along with the others."

She would never see him again—her Iiwatsu, her love, the father of her child. Reality sank in. Burning hot tears rushed to her eyes and spilled over. A sob escaped her, which she quickly muffled. She did not want to wake little Pip; she didn't know if she could be strong enough to be a mother right now.

"Thank you," she said softly.

"I'm sorry, I am really so sorry."

"I know you are. You should go get some rest," she said, swallowing. "You must be exhausted."

"I will be back to check on you soon."

Tiger Lily sat in the courtyard, tears blurring her vision. Just when they had found love, it had been taken away. Tiger Lily curled up into a ball and squeezed her knees to her chest, muffling her sobs not to wake little Pip. She would never again feel Iiwatsu hug her, brush her hair, or see his smiling face.

How am I ever going to live through the pain of losing my best friend and my husband? Then a little cry came from her son at the foot of the bench, and she realized that she had to find a way.

CHAPTER 9

Lead the Way

"Tiger Lily."

Tiger Lily stirred from her heavy slumber. Thinking it was only a dream, she leaned over to peer at little Pip, who laid sound asleep, and then snuggled back into bed and the much-needed sleep her body was begging for.

Then she heard her name again. "Tiger Lily, are you awake?"

Tiger Lily recognized Peter's voice and hurried to the window. "Yes, I am awake."

"I am leaving today and I wanted to see how you were feeling."

Instantly Tiger Lily was reminded of yesterday's events and her heart was filled with sorrow. She wrapped herself in a blanket and made her way down the short staircase that led out to the courtyard.

"Thanks for waking me to say goodbye."

"I couldn't leave without knowing you were okay."

"We will be," she replied. "Maybe not today, but in time. Where are you going?"

"The village is in need of all the hands they can get. If you don't need me here, I would like to go and be of service."

I need you! Tiger Lily wanted to yell. But she bit her tongue. She didn't want to be selfish in a time like this.

"Your father will be home any day; I want to be there when he returns."

"Father!" Tiger Lily gasped. "Peter, please come tell me the minute he gets home. I miss him so much!"

Tiger Lily could feel the tears welling up again. Besides Pip, he was the one person she had left in this whole world who loved her.

"I will, I promise," vowed Peter. He reached up to take hold of Tiger Lily's shoulder, but quickly turned away and was gone.

Many long nights had passed since Peter left—long nights left alone for Tiger Lily to grieve and think about her dear friend and husband. But being with her people in Neverland helped her, for all around her, she was not alone in her grief. Each family was missing a daughter or a son, a mother or a grandmother. Some children were left orphaned and some women were left childless. It was a devastating time; she could not stay in her grief knowing that the despair of others was just as great, if not greater.

Tiger Lily refused to allow herself to fall into the pattern of isolation that she had lived in the past. She kept her mind preoccupied during the day by helping out around Neverland, cooking and caring for the babies, and her evenings were spent sitting with the elders. In as much anguish, unease, and displacement everyone felt, life still had to go on. Food needed to be hunted and harvested, clothes and shoes needed to be made and repaired, and children needed to be reared and raised. Death waited for no one. Tiger Lily took great comfort knowing that her father would be coming home soon. He was the one person who could bring them safely out of this and back home to their beautiful shores and salty sea winds.

The day had finally arrived when Peter and the Lost Boys returned. Tiger Lily would finally hear news of her father! A mass of people gathered in the courtyard awaiting Peter's update.

"It seems as though the worst is over," Peter announced. The crowd let out a cheer. Peter continued with his news that the dead had been burned and the sick were on the mend. "There have been no other cases reported among the helpers in over a week," Peter added. "But it is not yet safe to return; you must wait until the chief gives the order."

Finally, mention of my father.

"I have had words with the chief," revealed Peter. "But I cannot relay any further updates until the grand council has met. Since time is of the essence, we must meet now."

The few remaining members of the grand council began making their way to the feast hall while the others continued to celebrate the good news.

"Peter!" Tiger Lily called out. But Peter did not turn. "Peter!" This time he turned and acknowledged her with a nod as he made his way into the feast hall already in deep conversation with the elders.

Tiger Lily was left again to wait. But this time she didn't dare leave. Her anticipation for news of her father was too great; she feared that if she left, she may miss the opportunity to speak with Peter.

Hours passed and still no one had come in or out of the hall. Little Pip was fast asleep in her arms when Tiger Lily finally heard the once muffled voices now audible in the near-empty courtyard.

One by one each tribal member filed out, and each looked at Tiger Lily with a sincere look and sorry smile. When it seemed that all the members were out, Tiger Lily was panic-stricken as Peter did not emerge.

Did I miss him? Did he leave through the back to avoid me? She rushed through the closed door to find Peter sitting at the far end of the table, staring into the fire.

"Sit," said Peter without taking his eyes off the flames. He knew her well enough already to know that she would be waiting. "You should have been invited to the meeting, seeing as you are next in line as head of your tribe in the absence of your father," he apologized. "Next time we meet, I will make sure that you are in attendance. But for now, I think it's best that you and I have this conversation in private."

Tiger Lily listened intently as Peter revealed what Chief Great Little Big Panther had learned.

"By the time the chief reached the south, he had seen more death and devastation than he had seen in all the wars in all of his time. Whole villages had been burned to the ground. People lay dead among the trails and pathways and the smell of death was thick all around him."

Tiger Lily sat in silence, listening.

"When he reached the village of Chief Talking Raven, it had already been abandoned. They came upon a man looting through the tipis. They approached him with caution, as he appeared to be a white-skin and they didn't know if he was armed. But when they saw that he was so inebriated he could barely walk, they approached him. When the man saw them he said, 'I thought we killed the lot of you. That was the best method of mass destruction we ever used. Hell, we even outsmarted the British army. They couldn't kill the amount of Indians that we could and we did it without a single gun.' They brought the disease into the villages using blankets."

Tiger Lily gasped. The blankets—the gifts that they had given.

"Your father tied him to a tree and when he sobered up, he was tortured until he revealed everything he knew." Peter paused for a moment and took a deep breath, "Tiger Lily, Captain Hook is alive. He managed to survive the waters that night at Mermaid's Lagoon and he has been plotting his revenge ever since."

The news that Hook was still alive was not as shocking as finding out that it was he who was the cause of all the death that surrounded her. Tiger Lily's mind worked overtime, sorting through all the details. "So that was him near our village during the potlatch?"

"Yes, Tiger Lily," Peter confirmed. "He was somehow able to inject this disease into the blankets, which he then traded with some of the tribesman travelling in from the west. Many of these blankets were then used as gifts, so this would explain why the western tribes were hit the hardest and the earliest. They don't know how he did it or where he is now. But we can be certain that he is not too far and that he will come back to finish what he started."

"Oh my... How can this be?" Tiger Lily murmured, her mind trailing off. *How could anyone be so cruel and have so much hate?*

"As long as you all are here you are safe. They still do not know how to find us."

"If the worst is over," Tiger Lily reasoned. "Can't my father and the others come here too? I'm sure it isn't safe out there for them—"

"Tiger Lily..." Peter interrupted. "There is more."

Peter closed his eyes and lowered his head. "Your father will not be coming to Neverland. He has fallen ill with the pox."

This news struck Tiger Lily with an impact far greater than the shocking news of Nascha, Iiwastu, and Hook all combined. As Peter continued to talk, the words seemed to fade out as Tiger Lily fought to remain conscious.

"He had withstood this disease for a long time—I thought he was strong enough to fight it, but eventually it got to him as well. I'm sorry, Tiger Lily. I didn't want to hide it from you. I need you to prepare yourself."

Tiger Lily stood up. "I need to see him."

He shook his head. "I'm sorry, you can't."

"I need to. I have to tell him I love him."

"He knows you do."

"I NEED TO SEE HIM!" Tiger Lily yelled. "I need to hear his voice. I can't lose another person in my life this way, without being able to say goodbye! I can't!" she cried.

"He will not be happy with me. But I think there is a way. Come."

When they reached the shores of her village, Peter draped a large heavy cloak over her head, the hood nearly covering her whole face.

"Peter, I can't see."

"And it is better that you don't," he answered. "Come, we must move swiftly before anyone sees you."

They scurried up toward her father's hut with Tiger Lily trying to peek out to catch a glimpse of her village. A sliver of a view was enough. Tiger Lily stopped dead in her tracks and pulled the hood off. She could not believe what she was seeing.

There was nothing left of her village—only burning and smouldering piles of wood where huts once stood. Of the masses that once covered the vast land of the largest tribe of the west, only five or six huts remained. At the village centre, a few men piled debris and tended to the fires that had been burning all night. The great hall that had been resurrected for her son's potlatch looked darker in this light. All the windows had been covered up to contain the disease and it was now clearly a house for the dying.

"Come, Tiger Lily, cover your head. We still don't know how this disease is spread—it's possible it could still be in the air."

Tiger Lily tucked her head back into the cloak and allowed her tears to flow freely as they made their way to the highest point of the valley.

When they arrived, Peter took Tiger Lily around the back of the hut. There he called out to the ailing chief. "Chief Great Little Big Panther, it's me Peter, can you hear me?"

"Peter, where are you? I cannot see you."

The sound of her father's voice reverted Tiger Lily to a child all over again. She felt a ball being lodged in her throat as she fought to contain her emotions.

"I am outside. I cannot come in right now."

"Father?" called out Tiger Lily, unable to hold back.

There was a long pause. The stifling of tears could be heard in his voice. "Tiger Lily, what are you doing here? Where is Pip?"

"Pip is fine, Father. He is back on Neverland," she answered, though each word felt like tiny knives in her throat. "Peter has been taking good care of us; we are all safe and well."

"Tiger Lily, you shouldn't be here."

Tiger Lily couldn't speak, finding herself struggling to hold back tears. Chief Great Little Big Panther was silent, too, undoubtedly holding back his own emotions. Finally he spoke.

"I want you to know that I am going to beat this..." He paused for air. "I'll get that Hook once and for all."

"I know you will, Father," she assured him. "And when everyone gets well, we will rebuild what we lost." Tiger Lily fought back the shakiness in her voice with all the strength she could muster. "But Father, in the meantime, I want you to know that we are all safe and well and Peter won't let anything happen to us...and I love you very much." A sob escaped her throat.

Through labouring breaths, Chief Great Little Big Panther shared a story with his distraught daughter. "When you were born...I wanted to name you Little Panther...even though we were saving that name for a son..." He paused for another few breaths. "Your mother wanted you named after a flower…so we chose the Tiger Lily…but what your mom didn't realize…" He paused again. "Is that the tiger is the greatest panther of all… She never knew…I won."

Tiger Lily let out a laugh through her tears. "When you see her, you better tell her that you tricked her," she said, smiling.

"You have to go now. It is not safe here," ordered the chief. "Peter, it is time for Tiger Lily to get back."

"Yes, Chief."

"I love you, Father," said Tiger Lily. "I will see you again." As desperately as she wanted to stay, she didn't want to worry him.

"I love you too," he replied. "And little Pip."

The walk down to the river was made in complete silence. Tiger Lily did not lift her head up to assess the damages further. She was too preoccupied with pain at the last words she would ever speak with her father.

Is this all a dream? Couldn't it just be a dream? The ache was unbearable. Each breath that held back her tears felt like a stake being driven into the middle of her chest.

When they reached the misty shore, Tiger Lily finally looked up at Peter. "Could you stay with him? I don't want him to be alone."

"Of course," Peter answered.

Tiger Lily embraced Peter tightly in her arms. "Thank you."

She climbed into the boat with the Lost Boys to head back to Neverland. As they sailed away from her home, she gazed at the fires lighting up the coast line. *It's so pretty in the night.* She wished it could stay this night forever.

Chief Great Little Big Panther died that morning with Peter at his side. The Lost Boys burned his hut and burned him along with his horse atop the highest hill. His funeral was not the traditional funeral of a chief, but Peter made sure that Tiger Lily's father was adorned in his best garments and a speech was read aloud as he ascended into the spirit world.

That night at Neverland they held a vigil for the chief and for all the fallen members of their tribe. One by one their names were read aloud as people wept and offered comfort to one another.

After the ceremony when the elders retired to the fire, they looked to Peter for answers of how to move forward. But this time Peter's response took everyone aback.

"I could only ever lead you all in the absence of your chief. But since your chief is alive and well, all direction must come from her."

The tribe fell silent. One by one they turned in the direction of Tiger Lily, who had not caught on as quickly and looked about in confusion.

"Tiger Lily is your new leader," said Peter, nodding at her. "All direction henceforth will come from her."

Tiger Lily could not hide her shock. *How could he do this to me? Clearly I'm not ready! Why can't he just make the decisions on behalf of my father and the people? What do I know?*

"But she has just lost her father," Peter continued. "We must allow her time to grieve. When we can leave the island and get everyone back home, Tiger Lily can assume her role. Until then, I move that all decisions be made by the grand council."

"Agreed," an elder sounded.

"Agreed," motioned another and another.

Tiger Lily, relieved and still speechless, nodded in agreement.

"So it is decided," declared Peter. "Until we are back in the village, the grand council will make all decisions."

The crowd applauded lightly to show their acceptance.

Peter got up from the fire and began walking away, Tiger Lily immediately at his heels. When they were far enough away from earshot, Peter stopped and turned to brace for what he knew was coming.

"Peter, how could you do that to me, ambush me like that and appoint me leader? I don't have the answers, what do I know about being a leader?"

"Tiger Lily, you *are* their leader now. I had to make sure it was known." Peter sat Tiger Lily down on a nearby bench and crouched in front of her. "I sat with your father as he lay dying. Our final conversations were about you. His faith in you was strong, Tiger Lily. He believed you have it in you to lead the people."

"I'm terrified." Tiger Lily's voice quavered. "What if I can't do it?"

"You can," Peter assured her. "He wouldn't burden you with this if he felt you couldn't do it, he loved you too much."

Peter was right. Her father would never place this large a responsibility on her if he wasn't fully confident in her, but she just was not ready to be a leader. She dreamed of the day little Pip would grow up to become chief, to learn from her father all his great teachings. She never imagined in all of her life that their time with her father would be cut short. It just wasn't fair. Nothing in this life seemed fair anymore. There was so much death and loss that the only thing that gave her any reason to continue was her son. She had to keep going—if not for herself, then for him.

Winter came and went and spring had found them once again, faster than Tiger Lily had wanted it to. It was now time to leave Neverland and return home, though she knew going home meant that her life would be thrust in the direction of change. She still did not feel ready. But like everyone else, she longed for the familiarity of their land. It was time to go home and rebuild.

As the weeks passed, the new huts came up. Each tribesperson was eager to get back to life as they knew it; they worked tirelessly day and night. Young and old pitched in to help. When Peter and the Lost Boys were not helping rebuild huts, they were out patrolling the waters and looking out for Captain Hook. The threat of his return was never too far from Tiger Lily's thoughts. But she refused to live in fear—there was just too much work to be done—yet at night, she would often find herself wondering about him.

What does he want? Does he want his revenge on Peter or the whole village? If he can devastate our people this way, what's coming next? She shuddered at the thought. Tiger Lily had never known of a human being that was capable of such hate, and it terrified her. And eventually the anxiousness she felt at nights was beginning to find her during the day.

When is he coming to take his revenge? she wondered. Tiger Lily didn't know when, but she had a dreadful feeling it would be soon…and she was right.

CHAPTER 10

The Storm Sets In

The days and nights that followed seemed methodological. The Piccaninny villagers continued to wake up with the sun and work until they saw the moon. As the days wore on, an unsettling silence began to blanket the village. Everyone was worried about Captain Hook and when he would be back to take his revenge, but mostly, their spirits were breaking. Tiger Lily had not even the strength to smile. Among her fear was sadness, guilt, and shame. The only thing that kept her going was Pip. Had it not been for him, Tiger Lily feared she may have just given up.

Upon their return to the village, Tiger Lily had assumed her title as leader; however, the role had not yet been fully relinquished. When the grand council met, they engaged in talks of how they could keep their people safe if Captain Hook were to return. Tiger Lily had yet to be called upon to make any decisions and most of the time not even asked for an opinion. But she didn't fight it; she couldn't help but to feel a failure. *I'm letting Father down by not being the leader he believed me to be.*

The grand council made the decision that if Captain Hook were to return, they would flee to Neverland. Tiger Lily listlessly agreed, though she knew that it would not have been the course of action that her father would have chosen. Her father would have stayed to fight. At this very moment, Chief Great Little Big Panther would have had his men working from sunup till sundown procuring weapons and devising plans. But Tiger Lily could not give that order. She could not be responsible for more death had she ordered them to fight a war they were in no way prepared for. Their weapons had been burned along with most other items they feared may have been affected by disease. The surviving villagers were also weakened by fatigue and famine, and in number. No, Tiger Lily would not push for war. They would flee to safety and try to remain alive.

Tiger Lily stepped out of her hut into the darkness. It was not quite morning but she had already been up for hours. The unsettling fear was growing and she could not shake it off. As she made her way about her area getting her fire ready, the darkness began to thin and morning was ascending on the village. Tiger Lily sat down with her tea in front of the fire and stared deeply into the flames, allowing her mind to trail off.

In her daydream Tiger Lily found herself in the clearing where she spent much of her youth. There she was, leading her tribe into battle. But instead of looking out at them eye to eye, Tiger Lily gazed down on herself and the others. She didn't recognize herself. She was tall and womanlike, and her look was fierce and bold. Her long black hair was not tied back in the two braids she wore every day, it blew wildly around her face from the strong winds. Tiger Lily was captivated by the brave woman who bore recognition of herself only by her eyes.

Then she saw herself open her mouth and out came a piercing war call that rang so audibly in her ears that it jolted her from her trance. She woke to find beads of sweat trickling down her face and her heart beating rapidly.

Tiger Lily panted, trying to regulate her breathing and then, just as in her daydream, she heard the call again. She looked around the quiet village. The call was coming from Elder Blackhawk. The short, stocky man was running from the ceremony grounds atop the hill. Almost all at once, the villagers emerged from their huts.

Without hesitation, the men jumped up on their horses and sped off in the direction of the hill and Elder Blackhawk. The women scrambled in panic, scooping up their children and ushering them inside.

Tiger Lily saw the elders approaching. "What do we do? What is happening?" they called.

But Tiger Lily did not know how to answer them. She didn't even know the answers herself. *Where is Peter?* she thought, frantically looking around.

Then she saw it: From the hilltop where her hut stood, Tiger Lily had a view of the open ocean, and there in plain sight were two large pirate ships docked on their shores. Tiger Lily looked down toward her village. The pirates were already there.

The pirates began setting fire to the huts and the trees all around them. Villagers began fleeing into the woods, running for their lives.

"GO!" yelled Tiger Lily to the elders. "I have to grab Pip, run into the woods!"

The elders fled into the trees as Tiger Lily rushed into her hut to grab her son. She snatched him out of his bed and ran out the door without even a blanket to cover him.

Tiger Lily ran furiously down the path, following her feet to the place her body instinctively took her. But when she came to the clearing, she realized too late she had just come to a dead end. Tiger Lily turned around to escape back down the path—but to her horror, she found herself face to face with Captain Hook and his band of pirates.

Tiger Lily screamed in sheer panic. She was all alone with Pip as Hook and his men spread out to block every possible escape. Slowly the tall, dark figure made his way toward Tiger Lily as she was forced further back toward the edge of the escarpment.

Terrified, she turned around. Panic had come over her knowing there was no way out. The only escape was down into the water. Clutching her son tightly, she looked over the edge at the raging waters below. There would be no way that she and Pip would ever survive the fall. Even if they did, the currents would surely drown them or throw their defenceless bodies against the rocks.

Tiger Lily turned back around to face Hook. *Do not show him your fear.* She was once again at the mercy of Captain Hook with no help in sight. She clung firmly to her baby as Captain Hook made his way even closer toward her.

"I came to get my revenge on Peter, but this is turning out to be much more fun," Hook said, not breaking his gaze on Tiger Lily. "I know how he cares for you—and who can blame him with beauty such as yours?—but before he dies by my hand, I want him to have lost all that he cares about first."

With each word, Hook came closer and closer. Tiger Lily looked around frantically for a sign of anyone, Peter or her warriors. *Where are they?*

"Your father was a fool to have hidden him, now look what he has done. Not such a great leader after all."

"You know nothing of my father!" Tiger Lily snapped. Even faced with death, Tiger Lily was forever devoted to her father's good name.

"Still the feisty one, aren't we?" he quipped. "I've had enough with you. I didn't come here to play your little games."

Captain Hook had moved in so close to Tiger Lily that she could feel his breath on her face as she stood at the edge of the cliff, struggling to maintain her balance.

"And I didn't come here for Peter either," he snarled. "I know exactly where that little fool is. I came here to take my revenge on him and I'm going to show him what real revenge looks like."

Captain Hook grabbed Tiger Lily by the neck and squeezed her so tight with his large hand that she had to fight for air.

As Tiger Lily battled to remain conscious, she could feel her grip on little Pip weakening. Then she felt him being ripped from her arms as the hold on her neck was released.

"What are you doing?" growled Hook to his companion.

Mr. Smee stood shakily, holding the crying baby in his arms. "I was afraid he was going to, to fall...in," the scared little man stammered.

"Afraid?" he scoffed. "Grab her!" Hook ordered his men. "What are you afraid for?" he said, turning his attention back to Mr. Smee. "Are you afraid for this child?" Captain Hook peered down at the crying baby in Mr. Smee's arms.

Mr. Smee remained silent and motionless, watching fearfully as his captain turned his attention fully to the child.

"Should we take him with us?" asked Captain Hook.

"Sir, I don't think..."

Captain Hook bent down slightly and snatched the baby from his arms.

"NO!" Tiger Lily screamed. She attempted to break free from her captors but their hold was too tight.

"Mr. Smee, how is this look on me?" asked the captain tauntingly to his quivering partner. "Do I look dashing as a father?" A sinister smile spread across Captain Hook's face.

Even Mr. Smee and the others could not hide the look of terror at the sight of their master handling the small child.

"Sir..." Mr. Smee began bravely. "I don't think sea life is any place for a child, wouldn't you agree?"

"Whaaattt?" The captain dragged out his question. "You don't think I would make a great dad?" Captain Hook's smile had disappeared from his face, replaced with a dark, menacing stare.

"I didn't mean it that way!" Mr. Smee pleaded in a trembling voice.

Captain Hook allowed the baby to flop over in his arm as his rage began to rise. He turned on his heel away from Mr. Smee and Tiger Lily, who was still powerless to break free. Ignoring her cries as if he didn't hear them at all, he walked back toward the edge of the escarpment with the baby under his arm.

Captain Hook stood at the ridge and stared out into sea, holding the child loosely at his side. He ignored Tiger Lily's piercing screams to let her son go and Mr. Smee's calls to get his attention.

The raging winds roared with fury over the clearing, threatening to blow to the ground anyone one in its wake, but Captain Hook did not budge. He raised the baby with both arms in the air until he was staring eye to eye with Tiger Lily's precious son. With a glare in his black eyes, he then snarled at the child, "I hate babies!"

Then, without warning, Captain Hook released his hold and let go.

Tiger Lily screamed as she saw her child disappear out of sight. She fell to the ground and the world went black.

CHAPTER 11

Raging Waters

Six Months Earlier

The winds howled in the night as the dark grey waves pounded the side of the pirate ship. Mr. Smee gripped the steering wheel so tightly that his stubby little fingers blistered and bled. His master stood at the mast of the giant ship laughing into the storm, barely hanging on as the crewmen clung to the railings for dear life. The ship bounced violently through the rough waters in the middle of the cold ocean. It had been months, possibly even a year since any of the men had stepped foot on dry land.

After Hook's lifeless body had been pulled from the grotto, the badly wounded captain refused to leave the waters. His life came close to ending that night at Mermaid's Lagoon, and no one but Mr. Smee knew how much the attack had actually weakened him. Back aboard the ship, Hook confined himself to his bedchambers attended to only by Mr. Smee. Every day in the privacy of his dark room, Mr. Smee would lift the captain out of bed and assist him in his attempts to regain movement. The knife Chief Little Big Panter lodged into the captain's back left him unable to walk, but Hook, although broken and battered, seemed fuelled by the prospect of revenge. With each day that he regained physical strength, his mental anguish was heightened. This was not the same man Mr. Smee set sail with so many years ago. That person was long gone and perhaps buried so deep that he would never be that man again.

Over the long cold months at sea, the captain grew more and more sinister and his hunger for revenge had turned him mad. Mr. Smee and the remaining pirates lived each day aboard the ship in constant fear of his unpredictable outbursts. If provoked in any way, the captain would fly into a fit of rage and would not hesitate to throw a man overboard at even the slightest misstep. Some days the captain would revert to torturing his men if someone so much as laughed too loud or spoke when the captain was trying to think. Hook was in a constant state of plotting his revenge.

Mr. Smee suspected that any reservations Hook had of how or when he would take his revenge was put off out of fear of the Indians. As long as Peter was being protected by them, there was no way Hook could get to him. There were far too many of their warriors and now only a handful of pirates. Mr. Smee noticed a pattern of Hook's mad ramblings that often involved wishing he could massacre them all, which made him even more anxious.

"Captain," Mr. Smee said timidly.

"What!" snarled the captain.

"We think, or I feel," he stammered, "that we should dock at the next port and replenish our supplies." It had been a long time coming but Mr. Smee finally had built up enough courage to speak up for the pirates who were growing weak and manic from being out at sea for so long. "I saw land back east and, well, we could stock up enough food and ale for months," Mr. Smee finished, hoping the speech he had been preparing for so long was enough.

"All right, we could use some more men, too. These ones," Hook said loudly, "are becoming too old and weak. I should just throw the lot of you overboard and replace you all!" he yelled over to the pirates, who were all trying their hardest to avoid any eye contact or distracting movement.

The pirates docked at a port on the shores of southwest Asia, as they quickly learned. Each of the men were genuinely surprised to find out they had come this far.

Captain Hook let out a hearty laugh and looked over at Mr. Smee. "I guess I ruined their plans of escape…even I wouldn't want to be left alone on these shores."

Mr. Smee turned to look around at the faces of the pirates who were huddled together like children, pushing each other to take the first step off the boat. Thoughts of leaving had deserted Mr. Smee so long ago that it had not dawned on him that the pirates may have been considering it. But in that moment, Mr. Smee realized that many of the men must have wanted to use this opportunity to escape, and now this idea was sadly out of the question.

The men clamoured into the first parlour that they found and immediately saw their spirits rise as they began to down the ale and gallon bottles of wine.

On the other end of the parlour, Captain Hook seated himself behind two men who were talking rather loudly with the bar owner. The men intrigued the captain; they both had fiery red hair similar to Peter's and thick wiry beards. Both men spoke with such a thick accent that one had to listen very closely in order to make out what it was they were saying.

The two men, it was revealed, were bounty hunters who had tracked their prisoners all the way from Ireland. Their story would reveal that an Irish slave owner who had tortured his slaves to their breaking point had been murdered in the most appalling way. The slaves concocted a poison and injected it into their master's clothing. When the master went to dress, he became infected with a deadly pox and died a slow and tortuous death, but not before sending a small plague through his tiny village.

"It wiped out the lot of them, it did," said the one Irishman, who had been doing most of the talking.

"If no one took notice that only the slaves survived," piped up the other. "Maybe they woulda gotten away with it!"

"Aye," the first one said. "They escaped into the woods I heard. But when anyone gets too close, the drum beats so loudly that no one dares go any farther."

"Well what brings you here to this port?" asked the tiny Asian owner, clearly enthralled by this riveting story.

Captain Hook leaned in a little closer.

"Well, two of the men escaped. They worked in the home."

"Yeah, witch doctors," the other man laughed.

"We chased them all this way. They nearly made it home, but we caught up with them just in time," the drunken man said proudly. "We got them in a cage out back. Gonna collect us a handsome reward once we get home...I'd say we might even be heroes."

The men laughed and continued to drink their ale and boast about their plans to spend their gold.

Captain Hook sat for a moment longer and then quietly got up, careful not to disturb the tales of the two drunken Irishmen. He walked over to Mr. Smee and whispered in his ear, "Put your book down and follow me."

Mr. Smee knew better than to question even the smallest of commands and followed the captain outside as he rounded the back of the parlour.

There, true to their words, was a cage that housed two very scared African prisoners. The captain looked pleased. He turned to Mr. Smee. "Go get two of the strongest men and bring them out here. If they cause a scene, I will cut their tongues out."

Mr. Smee dashed out of sight without a word.

"What are your names?" asked the captain.

The men were silent as they looked upon the tall slender man with a menacing brow.

"I know you understand me, I would hate to think you are deliberately ignoring me," said the captain, seemingly enjoying the opportunity to taunt some new bodies. "I'll ask you again, what are your names?"

"I am Raigon and he is Omosseau," said the older prisoner, who had only a few years on the other.

"I see," said the captain. "So it is you two I had been unknowingly searching for. How peculiar... But don't worry," he continued. "It is not the bounty I want."

Mr. Smee returned with the men. The captain promptly ordered the men to drag the cage containing the prisoners back to their ship.

"I am going to in to fetch the others," he said to Mr. Smee. "If anyone dares to get in your way, kill them!"

"Yes, Captain," he answered. Mr. Smee turned toward the disgruntled pirates. "You heard the man. Move!" he ordered.

The captain walked back into the parlour, to the owner. "I would like to order one last pint of ale for each of my men for the road, and a bottle of your best brandy for these fine gentlemen right here," he said, pointing to the two Irishmen still deep in conversation. They were enormously flattered at the gesture. "Oh why don't we make it two bottles—you men are far from home. It's nice to run into kinfolk here in these parts."

The two men graciously thanked the captain and said their goodbyes as Hook rounded up his men to leave.

When Captain Hook and his men arrived back at the ship, he was delighted to see that the cage bearing the prisoners was already on board. He immediately ordered the ship to set sail.

"But Captain, we still have not gathered our supplies," Mr. Smee reminded.

"Don't worry," said the captain. "We will dock at the next port."

Captain Hook seemed to be in good spirits; he even encouraged the men to keep drinking well into the night.

Mr. Smee, on the other hand, knew his captain all too well. He watched his every move and when the captain made his way to the cage carrying the prisoners, Mr. Smee followed right behind him.

"So I hear you two single-handedly wiped out an entire village?" questioned the captain.

The men were again silent.

"I want to know how you did it," demanded Hook.

Omosseau spoke to his elder in their language.

"Mr. Smee, open this cage please," Captain Hook requested rather politely. "I want to show our new guests what happens when someone disobeys me on this ship. Jacques, come!" he called out, summoning over one of his younger pirates. "Jacques, do you speak another language?"

"Yes sir, I speak French sir."

"I see," said Captain Hook. "Would you ever speak in French around me so that you could hide things from me?"

"No sir, Captain sir."

"And if you did, Jacques, what do you suppose I would do to you?"

"Probably throw me overboard sir," the young inebriated pirate laughed.

"Like this?"

Captain Hook lobbed the young pirate overboard into the frigid black ocean waters, his cries deafened by the sound of the loud party still going on.

Captain Hook turned his gaze over to Raigon. "I am going to get a good night's rest. You are not a prisoner on this ship and are more than welcome to jump into the freezing water if you dare."

The two caged men were clearly shocked by the incident and did not utter a word.

"Mr. Smee will show you to the sleeping quarters. When I wake, I trust you will be ready to share your little secrets with me."

Mr. Smee opened up the cage door and showed the men around the ship. But he did not leave them alone. Mr. Smee kept a close eye on Captain Hook's "prisoners" all night long, out of fear that they might actually just take the risk of jumping into the ocean. He didn't know what Hook was up to, but he knew for certain that it was important to him.

It was midday when the rest of the captain's men rose from their slumber, including the prisoners. The captain ordered Mr. Smee to bring the two guests down into his bed chambers.

"I am going to get right to the point here," the captain began, staring only at Raigon. "I know that the two of you were involved in the slaying of your former master and his entire village, and I also know that you disguised this death trap inside his clothing."

Mr. Smee's eyes went large.

"I want to know how it was done," the captain ordered.

Raigon glanced to his side at Omosseau, who was pleading with his eyes for him to keep silent.

"If you can successfully share this secret, I will not only grant you your freedom, I will take you to your home shores myself."

Omosseau piped up. "What is it that you intend to do with this poison?"

"That isn't any of your concern."

"But it is," he interjected. "I watched this medicine take out a whole village. If it is let loose, innocent people will die."

"Why do you care about innocent people now? You didn't care when you took out a whole village."

"That was an accident," Omosseau claimed. "It was only intended to stop a murderer."

"What if I told you the people I want you to kill are murders also?"

"I don't believe you," Omosseau revealed.

"I don't care."

Captain Hook and the dark man stood glaring eye to eye before Captain Hook stepped back. "What is it that you did before you became a slave? Your English is very good."

"I am not a slave. I never was!" Omosseau fired back. "I am a doctor. I am Dr. Omosseau Ranad." Omosseau's large eyes narrowed as he spoke and his voice was strong, full of conviction. "I worked as the slain Mr. Whitaker's family physician until his death. Before that I was the primary doctor in my homeland of Golla. And furthermore, I had no part in the demise of his family and village."

Captain Hook, tired of Omosseau, turned his attention to the older, shorter, and thinner of the two. "If he is not a man of the craft then I suspect you are. You would not have such a huge bounty over your head if you weren't, and lie to me you won't," he snapped. "If neither of you have what I am looking for, I will slice your throats before I finish my tea." The captain held up his arm to reveal his large hook to the men. "Now which one of you is it?"

"It is I," Raigon revealed. "I can grant you what you ask, but I will tell you with full transparency that I cannot grant your request. The medicines we require cannot be found in your land. They can only be found in my homeland deep in the jungles of East Africa."

"Do you take me for a fool, Mr. Raigon?" he asked, getting so close that they shared the same breath.

"No sir, I do not. And I do not care how you intend to use this poison. I only want my time on your lands to be over. I will do as you ask."

"Raigon!" gasped Omosseau.

"What do you care, Omosseau? I am tired. I am done. I want to go home. Why should you care what these people do to each other? We have seen so much death and cruelty. Don't you want it to be over?" Raigon pressed.

"Not like this," Omosseau answered. "I cannot have the blood of innocent people on my hands."

"Then don't. I will."

"It is decided then," Hook interrupted happily. "You will lead us to your shores. And you, foolish doctor..." he said, looking at Omosseau. "I will spare your life for now only because we could use a doctor on this ship, but if I find that you are of no service to me or my men, I will toss you to the crocodiles the first chance I get."

The ship was turned around and was now headed west, to another land no pirate had ever stepped foot on. Captain Hook did not chain the men back up and allowed them to roam the boat freely, but when they neared the shores of Africa, he was never without a plan.

"Captain," said Raigon, "where we are going is dangerous, too dangerous for you to accompany me."

"Of course it is too dangerous," he answered. "Mr. Smee here will accompany you. I will keep your doctor here until you return."

"I hope you don't mind having to return to your cage once again," Hook said sarcastically to Omosseau.

"I trust you won't take long," said Hook to Raigon. "He will not step foot out of here until you do."

"Yes, Captain," said Raigon, sounding defeated. "I understand."

"Good."

Omosseau was returned to the cage as several of the men suited up to leave, including Mr. Smee.

When the captain retreated to his chambers, Omosseau took his opportunity to make a final plea to Raigon.

"Run away when you can! Don't worry about me! You know what they are going to do with this poison. I would rather die than have the blood of these people on my hands."

"I cannot leave you," Raigon answered. "You have kept me alive all this time. I won't leave you to die at the hands of this devil."

"Raigon!"

But it was no use, Raigon would not turn around, and he along with Mr. Smee and a small band of men disembarked from the ship and into the jungles of Africa.

Omosseau stared out from his cage at the men making their way to the shore. For the first time in nearly six years his eyes were looking upon his beloved homeland. They had come this far and he would not even be able to taste the salty waters below him or let his bare feet sink into the crystal-white sand.

Several nights and days passed and there was still no sign of the men. Captain Hook grew agitated as he paced back and forth along the ship's deck. Omosseau did not know when the captain slept; he seemed to always be awake peering through his telescope into the dense jungle.

"Your foolish friend would not be so foolish as to run, would he?" the captain asked Omosseau.

I hope he did, he thought, though he did not dare speak his truth. He too was curious to know what had become of Raigon.

Hollering interrupted Captain Hook's furious glare at Omosseau, and he grabbed his telescope to peer out at a badly beaten Raigon and two dishevelled pirates making their way back to the ship, one of them being Mr. Smee.

Only two?

When they got on board, they immediately threw Raigon into the cage. "This man almost got us killed," the dishevelled pirate revealed. "We lost Tully and Sanky because o' this ere spook! There's demons and monsters everywhere in dis ere jungle. And 'e summoned them, I knows he did!" The pirate talked so fast he could barely catch his breath. "'E was chantin' some type a voodoo language da whole time."

"I was trying to ward them off!" Raigon claimed.

The men looked to Mr. Smee to either refute or support the pirate's story.

"It's true, Captain," said Mr. Smee, frightened. "There are spirits and animals the likes of which I have never seen before or would ever want to see again, but I can't know if his chanting called them on or warded them off, because those animals we seen would have eaten the lot of us, chanting or not."

"I would face a thousand Indians by meself before goin' back into dose woods," the other pirate added.

"Pipe down, you're safe," snarled the captain, clearly annoyed by the pirate. "Where are the others?"

"The last of the ingredients was blood from the heart of a silverback Gorilla," began Mr. Smee. "This monster was three sizes larger than a man. He ripped Tully in half with his bare hands, and when he was done with him he ravaged his teeth into Sanky and ripped out his neck."

The pirates were stone silent listening to Mr. Smee.

"I don't ever want to come across monsters like we seen in that jungle ever again. Let's get out of here!"

The captain's ship left the shores of Africa and headed northwest toward Europe. For the plan Hook was conceiving, he would need enough supplies to get them back over the ocean and another ship full of young foolish men looking for adventure.

The massive ocean waves tossed Captain Hook's ship about the sea like tiny toy boats that had been abandoned in a rainstorm. Raigon had been cast off into the new ship to concoct his potion, separated from Omosseau out of fear that the difficult prisoner would destroy the ingredients that were so challenging to procure. Why Hook did not do away with Omosseau was not known. Maybe it was out of necessity, as some of the new young pirates aboard the ship were ill with malnutrition, exposure, and fatigue—or maybe because his mind was now solely on revenge. The only certainty was that they were headed back to the land of the Indians and nowhere in between.

When the ship docked at the first port of the western shores of North America, the pirates were immediately drawn to the overwhelming influx of tribespeople travelling in droves to deliver gifts to the new grandson of Chief Great Little Big Panther of the Piccaninny Tribe.

Captain Hook's plan was now set in motion. Lavishly embroidered blankets were purchased and the poison embedded deep within. Gagged and shackled, Raigon was ordered to carry the blankets behind the pirates as they approached the travelling tribesman, offering to trade the blankets for anything they could, no matter how useless the item. Mr. Smee would accompany the men. The captain was not about to entrust just anyone with this crucial element of his plan, even if it meant endangering the life of his most loyal companion.

"We had a runner!" called out the infected Mr. Smee to the captain, standing at the foot of the gangplank. "Raigon tried to make off with the blankets, but was shot down."

"And the other?" asked Captain Hook, noticing that there should be one more.

"He abandoned us early this morning," Mr. Smee revealed. "We could not risk losing time looking for him."

A snarl spread immediately over the captain's face at this news.

"But you will be happy to know, Captain, that the blankets have been delivered," Mr. Smee added quickly. "I delivered them myself."

The captain looked clearly displeased by the events that surrounded this task. "The doctor shall sail with you on the boat." Captain hook glared over at Omosseau who was still in the cage. "I knew I kept you alive for a reason," he hissed at the man. "You will see to it that Mr. Smee survives."

I will not! Omosseau said in his mind, enraged and saddened by the news of his dear friend. *I will not lift one finger to keep even one more pirate alive,* he vowed.

For the next several weeks, they floated around aimlessly at sea, waiting for their plan to take effect. To Omosseau's surprise and equivocal disappointment, Mr. Smee did not take ill and he was reminded of his fallen friend's words: *If you are weak in mind or body, this disease will take you quickly, but if you are strong you can withstand it much longer.* Omosseau observed the odd little man to be weak in both mind and body and wondered why the disease did not take hold of him.

Once separated from Captain Hook, Mr. Smee spoke to no one. He kept to himself in the corner of the ship, staring blankly out into sea day after day. His complete withdrawal from the others was uncharacteristic of a seasoned pirate. Finally, over the course of the extended journey, Omosseau allowed his curiosity to gain the better of him and he decided to disturb the introverted pirate's self-isolation.

"Dare I ask where we are heading?"

"Your guess is as good as mine," answered the little man more swiftly than Omosseau had anticipated.

"You mean you don't know what his plans are?"

"No," Mr. Smee said flatly.

Omosseau waited patiently for Mr. Smee to offer up additional information, but he did not. Instead Mr. Smee continued to stare out into the water with the same faraway look he wore each day, remaining utterly detached.

But Omosseau did not give up. He too had been feeling fretful during this long journey; if anyone were to have any answers, it would be the person who knew the captain best. Omosseau needed to make some sense of this whole thing, for his own sanity and also to find reason to stay alive.

Over the next several days Omosseau continued to approach Mr. Smee, asking questions and pressing for answers. He realized quickly that it was not information he was seeking, as Mr. Smee gave that up without reservation, if he had it. Rather, it was an understanding of who Captain Hook was and why this ill-suited man was so devoted to him. It was not long at all before Omosseau was able to conclude that Mr. Smee was every bit a prisoner as he, but without the shackles.

As they wandered about the ocean, Omosseau learned all about the little old man with round spectacles. Mr. Smee took Omosseau through his life from the beginning of his friendship with Captain James Wallace II, right up to the day that brought them to their first sea voyage together.

Omosseau enjoyed these long conversations and began developing an affection for the man, although he was aware that the feeling was not fully reciprocated. Mr. Smee had yet to remove the shackles from Omosseau's ankles, though the keys to his freedom hung at his side during their conversations.

At nights when Omosseau lay awake under the stars, he wondered what plan Captain Hook had for his future, and if he was in his plan at all. He also wondered about Mr. Smee and whether or not he would have to force himself to hate the man who was so devoted to the enemy. But soon he would need to wonder no more.

The sound of rattling keys woke Omosseau from a light slumber on the deck floor where he often chose to sleep. When he opened his eyes, he saw a nervous Mr. Smee battling to unlock the shackles.

"We have no time to waste," he huffed. "Captain Hook is planning to attack the village this morning while they sleep. I am going to unlock you, but it is up to you to save yourself."

Omosseau looked around the boat. It was still dark and they were the only ones awake. *How does Mr. Smee know this news?* There was no time to ask.

"Do not leave until we dock," whispered Mr. Smee. "There is a tiny rowboat at the end of this ship. Here…" He handed him a blade. "Use this to cut it free."

Omosseau rushed to remove himself from the shackles and clapped Mr. Smee on the shoulder in gratitude, but Mr. Smee hurried away without looking up.

Within moments of his release, Omosseau heard the billowy voice of Captain Hook shouting out orders. Pirates began emerging from their sleeping quarters and running wildly about the deck, preparing to invade.

Omosseau grabbed the shackles and placed them near his ankles to give the appearance they were still on as the ship dropped its anchor. Like wild animals, the pirates charged off the boats and onto the shores near the Piccaninny village. The captain's orders echoed through the air instructing them to burn everything in their paths: trees, huts, boats—whatever they came across, they were to set it on fire.

Omosseau wasted no time getting to his escape. He tried to pull up the anchor to take over the ship, but he did not have strength alone, nor could he find a way to release it. *I have to try something else.* He ran to the other end of the ship and there, just as Mr. Smee had revealed, was a tiny rowboat tied to the rails. Omosseau took out the blade and cut it loose.

Before jumping into the water below, Omosseau took one last look over his shoulder in the direction of the Piccaninny village. Fire already lit the night sky and the screams of the innocent began piercing through the air.

Panting, Omosseau fiercely rowed away from the ship toward a rocky cliff nearby that jetted out into the water. If he could get around it before the sun came up, he could abandon the small boat and take refuge on land. But he would have to be careful not sail too close to the rock wall, otherwise the wind would surely send his boat crashing into the side.

Just as Omosseau was gaining momentum, rounding the cliff toward his freedom, he heard a scream from above. He glanced up to see an object hovering over the cliff. *That wasn't there earlier.*

Omosseau rested his oars to warrant a better look. And there, to his horror, in the dim light of the predawn morning he saw what appeared to be Captain Hook dangling a baby above the edge of the cliff. His eyes widened in horror. *I have to do something!* Grunting in effort, Omosseau began rowing feverously toward the wall, fighting against the violent waves in an attempt to position his boat beneath the infant.

And just when he had gotten as close as he could, just as Omosseau had suspected, Captain Hook released the infant from his grip.

Without thinking, Omosseau jumped into the frigid cold water. With arms stretched out in front of him, Omosseau was able to cushion the child's entrance into the water and for a brief moment, they both sank beneath the crest. Omosseau struggled to maintain his grip on the child, and when they rose up out of the waves, Omosseau swam back to the boat that was already beginning to float away. The baby sputtered in his arms, but thankfully didn't start crying.

Once safely inside the boat, Omosseau paddled himself and the sopping wet infant out of sight.

CHAPTER 12

When the Smoke Clears

When Tiger Lily opened her eyes, the air was thick and heavy and laboured her breathing. *Am I dead?*

Panic set in and her thoughts immediately went to her child. The last thing she remembered was Hook throwing her infant son over the cliff out into the sea.

Gasping, Tiger Lily ran to the edge of the cliff and looked out into the water. There was no sign of her son, no sign of pirates, no sounds of people, as if none of it ever happened. But it did, because she was alone on the cliffside with the remnants of a burned-out village behind her.

Maybe I'm dead? she thought again. But she knew she wasn't dead—if she were, surely she would not feel this much despair.

Tiger Lily fell to her knees and let the tears flow. Sounds escaped from her body that she had never heard before and she lay wailing on the cold ground in the sorrow that she was all alone in this world.

"WHY? WHY?" she screamed. "What have I done that has angered you so, that you would punish me to no end?"

Tiger Lily's anger welled up inside of her. *Why does Creator love everyone but me?* Not only did she lose everyone she loved, but she now felt abandoned and cast away by her Creator. The one who loved them all, except her, she thought.

People die all time—that she knew—and people die horribly sometimes. But never had she known anyone to be tortured and punished as she.

For a brief moment in time Tiger Lily had been happy. Little Pip filled her heart with so much love that she wondered how it ever could have been so empty. But now that he was gone, there wasn't anything that could keep her on this earth. She had nothing left.

Tiger Lily rose unsteadily to her feet and looked out over into the violently thrashing waters below. With Pip gone and her father gone, she had no reason to stay and pretend to be happy anymore. She wanted only to follow her son and perish in the water, even if it meant her soul would be stuck in limbo forever... At least they would be together.

Tiger Lily closed her eyes and lifted one foot off the ground. With a final deep breath, she allowed her body to drop forward...

But instead of feeling a free fall, Tiger Lily was yanked back with such force that she was thrown against the hard ground, several feet back from the cliff's edge.

Stunned by what just happened, Tiger Lily opened her eyes and tried to focus. A dark figure stood before her and she froze in fear that Captain Hook had come back to take her with him.

Tiger Lily clenched her eyes shut tight. *Creator, please make my death swift.* She felt his presence now standing over her.

"Miss, are you all right?" said a strange voice, close to her ear.

Tiger Lily opened her eyes to see a man with a face painted as dark as the night kneeling in front of her. She tried to scream, but her scream was muffled by the equally dark hand that clasped her face.

"Miss, do not scream," said the dark man. "I am not here to hurt you. I am here to help. I am going to release my hand from your face, but you must promise not to scream."

Slowly the man released his hand from Tiger Lily's face.

"Am I dead?" Tiger Lily asked as soon as she was able to speak.

"No, you are not dead," the man answered.

Just then Tiger Lily heard a cry that she recognized. Tears of hope filled her eyes.

"Pip?" she whispered. "Do you hear that?" she said to the man.

The dark man rose to his feet and walked to the large rock where Tiger Lily would sit when she visited this spot in her youth. When he walked away, she saw that he wasn't wearing a shirt, and his chest and back were as dark as his face. She stared.

The man reached down behind the rock and picked up a large bundle wrapped in what appeared to be his shirt.

But when he came closer, Tiger Lily could see that what was wrapped in his shirt was an infant...*her* infant.

"PIP!" she cried. Tiger Lily took her child from the dark stranger and saw a smile appear across his tiny face at the sight of his mother. "Pip, you're alive!" Tears filled her eyes, and for a moment she could not speak.

"How?" She turned to ask the stranger.

"I caught your child as he was coming over the rock."

"I don't understand," Tiger Lily said, bewildered. "Forgive me," she continued, "I should be thanking you first before questioning you." But before she let him speak she continued again. "Are you a spirit? Or a ghost?"

"I can assure you, I am not a spirit, nor a ghost," he chuckled. His laugh soothed her. "And you have every right to question, but first I think we need to leave from this open space; we are too exposed here. Captain Hook is gone but I do know that he is never too far away."

Captain Hook? Tiger Lily said to herself, looking over this strange man, wondering if she could trust him. *How does he know Captain Hook?*

But her questions would have to wait. He was right—they were not safe this close to the open sea. With Pip in her arms, Tiger Lily led the way back down the smoky path to what was left of the village.

The damages were extensive, more so than before. Most of the huts were burned to the ground, the huts that had been built only weeks before. As the sun rose, families began to emerge from their hiding places in the woods to assess what was left of their life.

When they saw Tiger Lily, everyone froze where they stood. She quickly remembered the painted man that followed behind her.

Tiger Lily turned to look at the dark man, and she too was taken aback by surprise. In the morning light she could see that the man wasn't painted at all. She quickly masked the look of shock on her face and placed her hand on his arm to show her tribe that he was not an enemy. His arm was strong and powerful, and as her touch lingered, his dark eyes turned to look into hers. She could see no evil in those eyes.

"What is your name, sir?" she asked.

"My name is Dr. Omosseau Ranad," he spoke loudly to the group, who had now formed a large circle around him. "I was taken prisoner by Captain Hook near my homeland of Africa, two oceans from where we are. He held me and my partner captive on his ship to serve as his doctor. Sadly my partner was killed trying to foil his plan of attack on your village. I was making my escape when I heard your scream from above my head. Captain Hook had thrown the infant over the edge and I caught him in the water below."

There was a collective gasp among the tribe.

"Yes," Tiger Lily said. "It is true. Captain Hook chased me up to the hilltop and ripped my child—your future chief—from my hands. His men held me down while he threw my son over the cliff. I was powerless to stop him. That is the last I remember before waking up to Dr. Ranad standing above me and returning Pip to my arms."

The tribespeople were stunned by this confession, and if it had been a member of another tribe, or Peter perhaps, he would have been given a hero's acknowledgement. But Tiger Lily understood their apprehension and the feeling of loss and distrust everyone was experiencing. They remained speechless as they stared the man up and down; even the remaining elders of the grand council and the most fearless warriors were at a loss for words. But to her surprise, Tiger Lily was not. For once she allowed her voice to come from within and spoke fearlessly.

"Dr. Ranad, I am Tiger Lily, daughter of the fallen Chief Great Little Big Panther. This is my tribe and this is my son Pip that you rescued from death. I am forever in your debt. Please accept my apologies for your friend. As you can see, we do not have much, but you are welcome to rest here and eat with us. Our dear friend Peter Pan will be returning soon from sea and I am certain that he may be able to assist you with finding a way to return to your homeland."

"Thank you, and please call me Omosseau."

Omosseau did not rest, though. He spent the day assisting the Piccaninny Tribe with what they knew to do—keep going.

They spent the morning putting out fires and gathering all the food that was left, and constantly looking out into the sea.

By the next day, the village had already resurrected tipis and shelters in record time, and they gathered together around the fire for a late meal. Now was the time for the conversation that was looming in everyone's mind.

In previous fashion, the elders, grand council, and other prominent members of the village would leave the fire to hold this discussion in private, but this was no longer an issue that was to be guarded, as it affected them all.

Elder Niikamich opened the discussion with a prayer thanking the Creator for sparing the loss of life and acknowledging that homes could be rebuilt but lives could never be replaced. He also thanked Creator for bringing the dark stranger to save the young child who would one day be chief.

With Peter still not back from sea, Tiger Lily knew that he would want her to assume her role as leader, but she felt a brief moment of hesitation. *What if I say the wrong words or give the wrong advice?* Then she realized that no one had the right answers, nor did they expect her to. What they needed was strength and encouragement, and that she could give. Tiger Lily's heart swelled with such gratitude for the return of her son, that she felt a renewed sense of faith in all that was to come.

"What are we going to do if Peter Pan is dead?" Elder Blackhorn said to the tribe, not making any attempts to dance around the difficult issues. "They went out chasing a pirate ship the day before the attack and have not been seen since."

The crowd grew sombre.

"The only thing we can do is pray for his safety and that he returns unharmed," Tiger Lily offered.

"And what will we do if Hook comes back?" a young tribesman cut in. "The best thing for us would be to flee to Neverland."

Elder Niikamich added, "We already had that in our plans, but there just wasn't enough time, and without Peter here, we don't know the way."

"And what if Peter doesn't return? Then what is to become of us? Hook will keep coming and burn our huts to the ground."

"Then we need to be ready to fight!" Swift Horse piped up.

"We don't have the numbers to fight him off anymore," said Elder Blackhorn. "We don't have the weapons either."

"What are we to do?" the young man asked.

"We should just take our children to Neverland," a young mother holding her child said. "Peter owes us that much. After all, it was him Hook was looking for in the first place!"

Tiger Lily noticed the crowd growing angry. "I think that we need to keep rebuilding," she said. "I have faith that he will be back, and I fear that fleeing to Neverland is only a temporary solution. As beautiful and safe as it is, we can't stay there forever and raise our children underground," she reasoned. "And we can't blame Peter—he could have never foreseen the level of destruction that could have come from this. No one could."

"May I interject?" Everyone grew silent as they stared intently at Omosseau, waiting to hear what the stranger had to say. "Your young leader is right—moving forward is important at a time like this. I have seen much evil in my life at the hands of others, but never in all my journeys across this vast world have I ever come across such evil in its purest form. Yes, he will be back if he has not gotten what he wants, and yes he will devastate your people in any way he can. This kind of evil has no end. If Peter Pan is alive, and if he has the means to stop him, then he should, but casting blame will not create any solutions."

"Then we must pray for his safe return," said the mother. "He is our only hope."

"Do you mind if I take a walk down to the shore to clear my head?" Tiger Lily asked Nayhani. Nayhani was Nascha's youngest sister and the only female of her family to survive the pox. Tiger Lily knew her loneliness all too well and brought her in to live with her and little Pip. "I'll be back soon."

"Take your time," said Nayhani, smiling, eager to cuddle little Pip in her arms. Nayhani resembled her older sister so much that it brought Tiger Lily much comfort to have her there.

When Tiger Lily reached the water, she was surprised to see that someone already had the same idea. She slipped off her shoes and tiptoed into the icy cold water to join Omosseau.

"Hello, what brings you here?"

"There's something about the water that brings me comfort," he answered. "Especially during times of confusion and uncertainty."

"You are very far from home," Tiger Lily acknowledged, letting her eyes wander over Omosseau, studying him. "I can't say that I know how you feel. But I do know the feeling of being separated from loved ones."

"You are a new leader, I take it?" Omosseau asked as they strode through small frothy waves together.

Tiger Lily looked at him, wondering if it was a good or bad thing that he noticed this. "Yes, my father was the Chief Great Little Big Panther, but he died during a pox epidemic, as did so many of our other village members, including my husband."

"Your child is still very young," he noted. "Your loss must still be near the surface."

"Yes, very much." She walked out of the water. "So much that I don't think I would be standing here today had you not rescued my son."

"I figured so."

Tiger Lily put her head down for a moment. "I just want you to know that I meant what I said. Peter is a great friend of mine, and when he finds out what you did for me and my son, I am sure he will help get you home." They walked along the sandy shore as she continued, "But I also know that he will not leave us until it is safe, so you may be stuck here awhile. I don't recommend trying to make that journey on your own. You will not find a ship nearby that could withstand the journey. Our lands are rough in terrain and the weather is unpredictable and unforgiving. We have lost some of our greatest warriors and hunters on these lands that they have lived their whole lives on."

Omosseau nodded in understanding. "I will stay and wait for the man they call Peter Pan. In my mind's eye he is more than a man. This I have to see for myself."

Tiger Lily laughed. "Peter is just a man."

"And so is Captain Hook," Omosseau pointed out.

They walked in silence as Tiger Lily pondered the analogy in her mind.

"Before my father died, I used to think he was invincible. My father was a great man, greater than Peter, more powerful than Captain Hook even… So I know now if he can fall, so can Hook."

"You are a very wise young leader," said Omosseau, his deep eyes seeming to stare through her. Tiger Lily laughed, brushing aside his compliment. She could not see in herself what he was seeing.

"If I were so wise then why don't I have any answers? I have no more answers than anyone else. I am just as scared as everyone."

"Leaders are not without fear," said Omosseau.

"Captain Hook seems to have no fear."

"If he had not had fear he would be here still, waiting for Peter Pan to return," Omosseau reasoned. "He has fear, everyone does… Even your father had fear."

Tiger Lily knew he was right. Even though this man had no knowledge of her father, she knew that his words rang true.

"I just wish that I could have all the answers the way he did. I know that I am not the leader that my people need."

"Your father sounds like a great leader, but he too was once a young man with many questions and many fears and, I am guessing, many doubts. Leaders are made, not born."

"I never thought of it that way," revealed Tiger Lily graciously. "In my mind he has always been fearless. But I guess you are right; he too was young once."

"May I ask…" said Omosseau, switching directions. "What of your mother?"

"She died when I was a child," Tiger Lily told her new friend. "I have very little memory of her. Sometimes I think I have memories of her but I don't know if they are real or if I created them from the stories told by my late grandmother and by my father."

Tiger Lily felt comfortable talking about her family to Omosseau. He spoke with such wisdom and insight about people he knew nothing about yet seemed to know thoroughly, and his manner was kind and sincere and not at all intrusive. She knew she would come to respect him and rely on him.

"He did not speak of her much," Tiger Lily continued. "I suspect now that it was too painful. She died giving birth to my brother; they both did not make it. Her name was Red Seneca and my brother was called Blue Bird Soaring High."

Tiger Lily smiled brightly as she spoke their names. It had been so long since she spoke them out loud; it seemed like a whole world ago.

"It sounds like your mother would have been the one person to have known the man behind the magnificent," Omosseau said, returning her large smile.

"Yes, I'm sure you're right."

"I am no leader either," he admitted. "I did what I could to help people survive, because that is what I know...how to stay alive."

As Omosseau spoke, his words of survival resonated deep within Tiger Lily.

"All I have been doing for so long is trying to stay alive, and there came a time while I was on that ship that I no longer wanted to stay alive. So I understood your mind when you were lost on that cliff. Though I have no children and do not know the loss of a child, I do know the loss of a family."

"I'm sorry you lost your family," said Tiger Lily, feeling the tears welling up in her eyes in sympathy. It was not so long ago that she lost Iiwatsu. "It must be so hard for you to be so far away from home."

"Yes. But I am here now and my death was not to be, and your son's death was not to be. So when I came out here this night, I was asking myself why?"

"Did you find an answer?" Tiger Lily asked earnestly.

"The only answer I have right now is that there is a greater purpose to fulfill. So we must go on surviving until that purpose is made clear. I'm sorry that it is not the answer you are hoping for, but it is the answer I know to be true."

"Thank you, Omosseau," said Tiger Lily. "You've been a great help."

He smiled and nodded. "Good night, young princess."

"Good night and thank you again."

At last Peter's ship sailed into the horizon, but as the vessel drew near, some villagers retreated nervously to the treeline, ready to flee in case he were no longer on board. Almost immediately Tiger Lily noticed Peter's red hair and called out the others that it was safe. They rushed to the shore to greet him.

Peter was shocked to see that their huts had been burned to the ground, yet he had happy news to share. Peter informed the crowd that they had sunk the pirate ship they'd been chasing and then slain all the pirates on board.

"That ship must have been a diversion," Omosseau disclosed. "It must have been sent out to distract you while the captain made his move."

"Who are you?" demanded Peter, striding up to the dark stranger.

Tiger Lily quickly stepped in front of Omosseau to Peter's shock. "Please excuse him, Peter, he means no harm. He is our friend."

Omosseau tried introducing himself to Peter, but was overtly dismissed.

Now that Peter was back, it seemed that a sense of normalcy had returned with him. Elder Niikamich called for an immediate meeting of the grand council to be held in the tipi of Elder Blackhorn.

As the small group gathered around the familiar fire, the elders filled Peter in on what had transpired in the short time he was away.

Peter asked, "What do you know of this stranger?"

Tiger Lily was quick to reveal her trust in the man who saved her son's life, although she could sense that Peter was still skeptical of Omosseau.

"He is very brave to have risked his life for your son, but I think he needs to be questioned further," Peter reasoned. "He spent much time on the boat with Captain Hook. Surely he gathered some knowledge of his plans."

Peter was right. Tiger Lily was allowing her emotions to cloud her leadership.

After the meeting, Peter and Tiger Lily approached Omosseau, who was seated comfortably in front of his fire. "Please sit."

Back in Omosseau's presence, Tiger Lily felt the same warmth and comfort that allowed her to have such trust in the stranger. She hoped that her impression of him was accurate and he was not harbouring any secrets or false information.

Peter started the conversation. "Could you tell us how it is you came to be a prisoner of Captain Hook?"

"And please," urged Tiger Lily, "do not leave anything out."

Omosseau recounted the tale of how they were captured out behind the parlour as their original captors drank inside.

"Why were you being held in the first place?" asked Peter. "Were you taken as slaves?"

"No!" Omosseau rushed to answer. "I have never been a slave. I was a personal physician for—"

"But how does a physician become a prisoner?" Peter interrupted.

It was clear that Peter's guard was up with their new guest. *Maybe I had been naïve not to question him further,* Tiger Lily thought.

"There was a large bounty over our heads," revealed Omosseau.

"Why?" Peter quipped.

"My companion Raigon and I were held responsible for poisoning the plantation owner that we worked for."

"Did you?"

Omosseau paused at length. "No, I did not."

"Did your friend?"

"Yes," he revealed with a sigh before continuing. "I was implicated in the act because I, as his physician, had close personal access to him."

"So why is it that Hook wanted you?"

"He used me as his physician."

"But you said you were a prisoner on board his ship," said Peter suspiciously. "Were you his prisoner or his doctor?"

"I was both," said Omosseau, staring at Peter now.

"Then try to help me understand," said Peter, his aggression heightening, "why two Irishmen would chase you that far for the murder of one plantation owner. It must have been some bounty on your heads."

Omosseau looked defeated. He stared long and hard at Peter before revealing his truth. "It was not just one man who died. The poison swept through the village and wiped out everyone."

Peter looked over at Tiger Lily. She could see in his eyes that something was very wrong. Tiger Lily felt her heart begin to pound. *This is it,* she thought. This was the moment when all her feelings of security would come tumbling down.

"You are right to question me," Omosseau said finally.

"I feel that you have not been fully transparent about what you know," Peter said. "But I did not want to question you in front of the others because they are already scared enough. Tiger Lily and I need to know what is it that you are hiding."

"Please know this," said Omosseau, speaking directly to Tiger Lily, "I never meant to hide anything or harm anyone."

Omosseau looked back at Peter and began his long tale. He took Tiger Lily and Peter back to his journey from the very beginning, where he studied medicine in Nairobi.

"I had just returned home to Golla to practice medicine for my people, until the Englishmen showed up and burned my village to the ground. They took all the strong men and women as slaves and left the young and the elderly to fend for themselves. My friend Raigon, who was also a doctor, but a doctor of another kind, convinced me to board the ship as physicians for the Englishmen so that we could watch over our loved ones. I agreed, but this did not last long. As soon as we arrived in Europe, all the men and women were sold at slave auctions. That was the last I saw of my brothers and sisters."

"What of your parents?" asked Tiger Lily.

"They died of age," answered Omosseau. "My mother when I was practising medicine in Nairobi and my father not long after I returned home to Golla."

Omosseau continued with his story, revealing that he and Raigon travelled by land to Ireland with the slave driver to work for his brother, who owned a large plantation. "It was there that I stayed the longest. Raigon and I watched as the slaves endured the most inhumane treatment of human life, until, of course, we met Captain Hook. The slaves begged Raigon to help them. To create a poison that would kill him so they would be free. Raigon agreed and created a poison using the last of the medicines we had brought from home. Even Raigon himself did not know the destruction that this poison would cause."

Omosseau glanced over at Tiger Lily, who was listening intently to the story. His eyes filled with sorrow for what was coming next.

"The poison was placed inside the clothing of Mr. Whitaker. When he put the clothes on, he was infected with an illness that covered his entire body in sores and puss that oozed out of every hole, even his eyeballs. The disease then ran through the village with everyone dying in the same horrid fashion."

"Just like the pox that tore through this nation and beyond," noted Peter.

"Yes, it was exactly the same," Omosseau confirmed. He looked at Tiger Lily, whose mouth had dropped open at this revelation.

"Did you bring this disease here?" she asked.

"Yes," he answered.

Omosseau told them how Raigon was forced to concoct the potion. That he had tried escaping in both Africa and here before the potion was let loose. That he had refused to have any part of making the potion or delivering it to their people even if it meant his death.

"I assure you, Tiger Lily," he pleaded. "I did not have any part in the destruction of your people. I give you my word."

"Is there anything more that you have neglected to tell us?" Peter asked.

"No, I have told you everything," Omosseau confessed. "But I feel that I should add that I have been around Captain Hook long enough to recognize the patterns of his current state."

"Go on," urged Peter.

"He wants revenge, but no matter how mad he is, he is fearful of failure. Since you have weakened his army, he will need to go in search of more men. This buys you time to devise a plan for his return. And he will return. He has not yet conquered what he wants."

"My death?" asked Peter.

"No," Omosseau said, to Tiger Lily's shock. "If he wanted that, he could have taken it when he lured you astray."

"Then what is it he wants?" asked Tiger Lily.

"I regret that I do not know. The only answer I can give is that he vowed to take back what you took from him."

Tiger Lily looked at Peter questioningly. "What did you take from him, Peter?"

Peter rose to pace in front of the dimming fire. "It could be many things. I took his ship, his treasures…his hand."

"His dignity," added Omosseau.

Peter nodded in acknowledgement at Omosseau.

"The others do not need to be made aware of this news," Peter said to Tiger Lily. "Thanks to your father, we were able to trace the disease back to Captain Hook and the blankets. I feel that if word got out about this, it would cause a manhunt for the wrong person," he said, looking at Omosseau.

"But he is right—the village is safe for now—and we will need to use this time to formulate a plan. I will be back in the morning." Peter nodded at Tiger Lily and Omosseau and left for his waiting men.

Omosseau and Tiger Lily sat in silence as he gave her time to process her thoughts.

"I do not know what to feel. Your disease has weakened our village and took from me my husband and my father. But you gave your freedom to save my son. I feel conflicted in my mind right now."

"Tiger Lily, when I said that I no longer wanted to go on, it was because I could feel the pain of loss that was caused at the hands of this man. I feel it still..." Omosseau's words again spoke deeply to her soul. "But like I said before, there is a reason I am still alive. He had many opportunities to kill me; he killed often and without hesitation. I don't know why I am in this strange land or I why I am here in this place with your people, but I will help in any way I can, to help you survive.

"In my home we had been raided many times, our villages burned to the ground, our people taken, our families broken. We have lived through wars; each time we have gotten back up and rebuilt just as you want to see your community do now. I vow to help you in any way I can."

Tiger Lily knew in her heart that she could trust him. She didn't know how she knew but she knew, even if Peter did not. It was not Omosseau's fault that their people had suffered, just as it wasn't Peter's fault. She welcomed his knowledge, his wisdom, and his presence. The next words came from deep within her heart.

"I trust you."

CHAPTER 13

The Heartbeat Drum Sounds

All through the winter Tiger Lily and her people worked tirelessly to rebuild their homes. True to his word, Omosseau stayed on to help in any way he could. To everyone's surprise, he was even more help than any of them could have imagined. Omosseau spent his days with the builders showing them different styles of building and different ways of binding; he was never insistent but only ever looked to help. The master builders welcomed his knowledge and the people were in awe of the sturdy new structures that were taking shape.

"Is that how your huts are made back home?" Tiger Lily asked, admiring their work. Her heart was filled with gratitude for Omosseau. It was not just knowledge of building he brought with him, but hope and strength as well. He had quickly become an integral part of their community.

"No," Omosseau chuckled. "They are far different from the huts back home. Back home we don't have to withstand the fierceness of this weather."

"Oh?"

"Back home, the heat is our enemy," Omosseau revealed. "These structures here, I learned to build in Ireland."

"But I thought you were a doctor?" Tiger Lily questioned.

"Indeed I was, but after a long day's work, anyone who could get away would go far out into the forest and build these huts for our people to come for a place of worship. Raigon and I would be there every day working to get these huts up for them. It was a long trek into the woods each day; we needed to build far enough away so that the music and singing was not heard."

"That sounds so very sad, that you had to hide your worship," Tiger Lily said, thinking of her ability to pray freely to the Creator. She couldn't imagine not having that luxury, and admired Omosseau's bravery.

"Yes it was, but it was also very beautiful and very much similar to here. With every beat of the drum you would fall further and further into yourself, into nature; it was the only place where we could feel a sense of home. These huts were also a place of new life. If the women could make it in time, many of them would come to have their babies in secrecy in these huts."

"Why in secrecy?" Tiger Lily asked.

"Because so many of our women were taken as concubines by the slave owners and overseers; it was never known if the child would be born of mixed race until birth."

Tiger Lily was grateful to Omosseau for offering up the stories of his home and his hardships so freely for her curiosities. She knew it couldn't have been easy and she respected him for it. Deep down inside, she could feel as if his heart was speaking directly to hers.

"And what of the child if it was born of mixed race, what would happen then?" she asked, to shift her focus.

Omosseau was silent for a moment as he reminisced in his mind. "That would be the decision of the mother," he revealed solemnly. "Babies were not as celebrated as they are here—not that they weren't loved or wanted, but it was not an environment that anyone wanted to bring a child into. Some days the work was so gruelling that they could barely find the energy to keep themselves going, so to bring a child into that world brought more fear than anything."

"My heart aches for those mothers," Tiger Lily said as she wiped away her tears. "Do you have any children?"

"No. regrettably I never did marry nor have children," he answered truthfully. "It was my dream after medical school that I would come home to Golla and raise a family, but that dream was taken from me quite quickly."

"I pray that you make it home someday and find a wife and have children," Tiger Lily said lovingly to her friend.

"Thank you. I believe in the power of prayer and I pray for that as well."

"If you like, we can pray together," offered Tiger Lily.

Omosseau accepted her offer, and each morning he would walk up the hill to her hut and lead them in prayer before they started their day. Omosseau would ask the Creator for strength and guidance for Tiger Lily and protection for her people, little Pip, and Nayhani. Tiger Lily would end their prayer asking that Omosseau would one day find his way home and be blessed with a family.

Tiger Lily felt stronger with him around. She learned from him every day and she loved how his wisdom did not just come from stories or from him showing her. The wisdom came from the answers to the questions he would have her ask of herself. Omosseau never provided her with his own answers, although she often tried to pull them out of him; instead, he would force her to search inside herself until her own answer came to light. Not only did this amuse Tiger Lily, but it made her feel important. When she was around him, she could tell that Omosseau never felt that she was not enough, the way she did when she was in the presence of the grand council. She felt safe with him. She was allowed to be fearful and that it was not considered a weakness.

Other than Peter, Omosseau was the only person in the village who knew how afraid Tiger Lily was to fail. How much she questioned her worthiness as a leader and how each day was a struggle to find courage. She had to be the rock that the people needed...but he was becoming the rock that she needed.

"Thank you," said Tiger Lily to Omosseau, who was kneeled in front of Pip testing out the rattling toy he had just fashioned for him.

"No trouble at all."

"No, thank you for everything," Tiger Lily pressed. "For helping us rebuild our homes, for listening to my fears, helping me with Pip... I know I've said thank you many times before for saving my son, but this time I want to really say thank you for everything you've done for all of us."

Omosseau opened his mouth to speak but no words came out. He smiled and put down his head. "You're welcome." He blushed.

Things had begun getting back to normal—at least as normal and normal could be. The daily bustle of men and women hard at work and children laughing and playing filled the air, although the children never strayed too far and the adults' faces remained guarded. It was spring once again and a time for new growth and new beginnings as young men and women were falling in love and making plans for new life. But this sense of comfort, Tiger Lily was triggered with a sense of unease. Captain Hook's presence had invaded her mind again.

Tiger Lily spent the day pondering her uneasy feeling. *How will I bring this up to the grand council without being prodded for answers to questions I do not know the answer to?* She knew they could not go on any longer pretending that Hook was not out there planning his next attack. It was time to call a meeting. No sooner had this thought entered her mind, Peter came rounding the corner with the Lost Boys behind him.

"We have just received news that Captain Hook plans to attack on the day of the Great Sun," he said, breathless.

Tiger Lily's fears were confirmed. "I will call a formal meeting of the grand council."

When she made her announcement of Captain Hook's plan to the others, the fear could not be concealed. The mere mention of his name threatened any sense of happiness and peace the council had managed to regain. But they could not fool themselves any longer. The looming threat of Captain Hook entered the minds of everyone at least once throughout their day. It was now time to carve out a plan for the people, as the attack was inevitable.

Elder Blackhorn opened the meeting by relaying to the council that he had tried without success to receive guidance from the spirit of Chief Great Little Big Panther, revealing that his spirit waited for his daughter to seek the answers.

Everyone turned to look at Tiger Lily in anticipation of a mystical answer from beyond. "You mean you spoke to my father's spirit and that is what he told you?!" Tiger Lily asked so eagerly that she nearly rose up out of her seat.

"The spirits do not speak to us as we speak to each other," Elder Blackhorn scolded, shaking his head in disapproval.

"Was that what you were waiting for?" asked Elder Niikamich in disbelief.

She could hear several people let out their laughter but she didn't dare look around out of fear that she would expose the tears welling in her eyes. This is exactly what she feared. Tiger Lily felt embarrassed and even more juvenile and ill-equipped for this role than ever before.

Tiger Lily remained silent for the rest of the meeting as they discussed plans and scenarios in case of attack. She listened half-heartedly to the suggestions, and when it was over she rushed back to her hut before Peter could stop her. She had been so humiliated that she couldn't bear to face him.

"Tiger Lily," Omosseau called from outside her door.

"Not now, please."

"Please, let me in," he urged. "Peter told me what happened and I want to help you."

For a moment she wanted to be angry with Peter for telling Omosseau, but then she realized that he only did it to help her. Omosseau always had the right words to say in moments of great turmoil, and Tiger Lily often told Peter how great of a help he had been to her. She opened the door to let him in.

"I feel like such a fool," she blurted out as he took a seat on the floor. Tiger Lily could not sit; she paced the room wildly.

"They speak of the spirits guiding them all the time, telling them what to do. I have not had one visit from my father or grandmother…or mother. I have never had spirits speak to me and send me the answers. Am I doing something wrong? Why do they not speak to me?"

"Tiger Lily, I am sorry that they made fun of your misunderstanding, but please don't allow their callousness to deter you in any way from seeking answers from your spirit guides."

"I'm such a failure!" she moaned, grabbing at her head.

"You aren't."

"You don't understand…" Tiger Lily finally took a seat. "There are so many teachings that I lack. So many teachings I pushed away and refused to take part in. When everyone else my age was learning the ways of our people and our ancestors, I was hiding away in my hut feeling sorry for myself… I went through this very dark time in my life and I missed out on so much, and there is no one to blame but me. I chose to wallow in my grief rather than to face life." Tiger Lily looked over at Omosseau to reveal her tear-stained face. "And I can't even blame them for laughing at me. I brought it all on myself." She brushed her tears away as if she had no right to cry.

"Don't be hard on yourself, Tiger Lily. You have had much to grieve for and no one can blame you for retreating into yourself during your time of loss."

His words brought Tiger Lily to shame. She lowered her head and continued to wipe away the tears that were streaming down. "If only you knew," she said quietly. "You would not see me as so worthy."

"How can I help you?"

Tiger Lily felt Omosseau's large hand gently grasp her chin. Her heart beat quickly at his masculine touch.

"It is going to be okay. You are meant for this, really you are."

Tiger Lily took a deep breath and nodded.

"We can receive messages and guidance from our loved ones who have gone on," Omosseau explained, "but not in the language you and I know. The messages come from the language of the heart. Listen for them in the stillness of your mind. Draw messages from what is placed before you when you are not seeing with your eyes or listening with your ears. The answers come from within."

Tiger Lily wiped the last of the tears from her cheeks and looked up at Omosseau.

"This may not be the answer you were expecting, but I can assure you, when the message comes to you, it will be as clear as any language ever spoken."

"Really?" she asked.

"Yes," Omosseau assured her. "It is up to you to quiet your mind and clear a path."

"I fear I have never been able to quiet my mind; it has tormented me so."

"You can," Omosseau reassured Tiger Lily. "They key is not to try so hard. Allow your mind to drift where it wants to go and not where you want it to go. It will take time and practice but you will get there."

Tiger Lily thanked Omosseau for his kind words and allowed herself to hope that what he said was true and that she were not immune to these messages. She needed to believe that she was worthy of such divine selection, as she felt it was all she had left.

The next meeting of the grand council was not as bad as she anticipated. It was agreed that they would each take three days to ponder the options that everyone had put forth: flee to Neverland, begin training all men for battle, or relocate the village inland and use Chief Great Little Big Panther's gold to trade for safety. Most seemed to push in favour of the first; however, as Peter reminded them all, the final decision would be made by Tiger Lily.

On her walk back toward her hut, she looked around at all the groups of people as they went about their day, oblivious to the perils of their leader's mind. Suddenly her attention was directed toward two men talking loudly coming up the trail behind her.

"Sweat lodge begins tomorrow at sundown. I am going early to get a good spot away from the rocks."

"How will the grandfathers speak to you if you are hiding in the corner?"

The men jokingly teased each other and continued on their way.

That's it! If she could get into the sweat lodge, maybe the grandfathers would speak to her and guide her way! She hurried up the hill to where Elder Blackhorn was directing his young helpers to put the finishing touches on the sweat lodge for tomorrow.

"Elder Blackhorn!" Tiger Lily shouted. "Can I talk to you please? I need to ask a great favour..." She ran up toward him, barely stopping to catch her breath.

"Can I attend the sweat lodge tomorrow?"

Elder Blackhorn looked alarmed at this request.

"I know women are not permitted to attend the sweat lodge, but I really need to go in. I have been searching for messages from our forefathers to guide my leadership of the village. And well...I feel that I am failing. Please, Elder Blackhorn, I'm begging you."

Elder Blackhorn looked at the sweat lodge and then back at Tiger Lily. After a few more moments of complete silence he spoke. "Are you on your moon time?"

"No."

"Be here at sunrise."

"But I thought the sweat lodge starts at sundown?"

"For the men!" Elder Blackhorn boomed. "You will go with the boys."

Tiger Lily opened her mouth to object, but stopped herself and instead thanked Elder Blackhorn for his decision. Even though she was the leader of their village until her son came of age, she too had to follow the sacred traditions and customs of their culture. Elder Blackhorn was providing her a great honour by allowing her inside.

While the village was still dark, Tiger Lily stepped out of her hut. She greeted the day with a deep inhale of the cool fresh air and made her way to the top of the hill, where Elder Blackhorn was already outside getting ready.

"Hello," she greeted him.

"Hmm." That was the extent of Elder Blackhorn's greeting.

"Thank you for letting me come," she continued. "I know it was a huge request."

"Don't die," he said.

"Okay…" said Tiger Lily, a bit taken aback. "I won't."

The other young boys started to make their way up the hill, chatting and laughing. When they saw Tiger Lily, they stopped and looked quizzically around at each other. Tiger Lily ignored their looks.

As they assembled inside the lodge, each boy took his place around the fire. Tiger Lily sat beside Elder Blackhorn and listened attentively as he gave his instructions and led them through prayer.

As he poured the water over the rocks, a wave of heat came blasting toward her accompanied by a loud hissing sound that rang through her ears. Tiger Lily remembered Omosseau's words and tried her hardest to quiet her mind.

As the time bore on, minutes felt like hours. She looked around at the young boys who in the beginning sat watching her, seemingly waiting to see what would happen. Each had trailed off into themselves and Tiger Lily felt like she again was the only one who didn't know what to do.

In the heat and the darkness, she battled with herself.

How am I supposed to connect with myself and with spirit? Why am I not a spiritual being like all the others? Why did I allow myself to miss out on so much learning? Why did I have to go through heartache in the first place? Why did everyone who was supposed to love me leave me when I needed them the most? Why do I now have to be an adult and take care of everyone? Why am I being punished for being a selfish girl?

More water evaporated over the hot rocks and she closed her eyes and took several deep breaths. She couldn't bear to look at the boys who were no doubt having a spiritual experience. She just needed to keep her eyes closed and wait it out. Quitting was not an option.

"I cannot tell you what to do," Father was telling Tiger Lily. He and Grandmother were sitting in front of Tiger Lily in his hut, all three of them unusually too close to the fire.

"You are their leader now," Father said gently. "Any direction must come from you."

"But can't you just tell me and I will direct everyone?" Tiger Lily pleaded.

Father laughed and looked over at Grandmother. "If you really need the direction to come from me, just ask yourself what would I have done in this situation. Then you will know."

Grandmother chimed in, "Yes, that is the answer. Go now and help them."

"No," Tiger Lily pleaded, "I'm not ready." She felt that they were dismissing her, as if she were asking such a silly question and they did not want to entertain the silliness anymore.

Then Father looked at her and said something that seemed off topic and nonsensical. "Don't forget to braid the sinew together when you thread your cradleboard. We had to learn the hard way, didn't we, Mother?"

They turned to look over at Tiger Lily's mother at the other side of the hut, standing with her back turned to them tending to a baby. She did not turn around, only nodded in agreement. Tiger Lily stretched her neck trying to get a clearer image of her mother.

"Your little arms would bust out the seams every time," Father continued talking to Tiger Lily. "Yes, braid the sinew strings together. Individually they are strong but together they are unbreakable."

"Cradleboard?" said Tiger Lily, getting frustrated. "Why are we talking about cradleboards? We are in the middle of a crisis and all they can talk about is—"

"Oh! It's starting to rain again!" Grandmother interrupted. "I thought you were getting that hole patched up?" Tiger Lily looked up at the ceiling of the hut as large drops of water began to splash down on her face.

As she struggled to open her eyes, she was startled to see five little heads surrounding her and Elder Blackhorn standing above her about ready to pour another basin of water over her head.

"She is awake," one of the boys called out.

"Help her up," instructed Elder Blackhorn.

The boys lifted Tiger Lily to an upright position where she sat for a few moments trying to regain her composure.

"I think we are done for today," Elder Blackhorn said with a sour look in her direction.

That night talking with Omosseau, Tiger Lily relayed the day's events. "Why was Mother so far away?"

Omosseau shared with Tiger Lily the most reasonable answer he could find. "The mind can only conceive what it has borne witness to. Your mother's passing was so long ago that you don't have memories of her voice and her interaction with you. The only sureness you have is how much she loved you."

Tears streamed down Tiger Lily's cheeks. She understood and wished that she had more control over her dream—or vision, or whatever it was she had. She vowed to herself that if she were ever to be blessed with another vision of her mother, she would run and embrace her.

It was the day before she had to give her decision to the grand council and she had talked with Peter and Omosseau numerous times, but both were guarded with their answers. It needed to be her decision, although she felt no closer to having made up her mind now than she was two days ago.

Tiger Lily walked down to the shore past the quiet happenings of the village. She observed the families talking together, children helping parents and grandparents, men and women working together. This was the first time Tiger Lily truly realized that all of these people, with their busy lives, looked to her for guidance and support, as young as she was. There was no way to escape her duties or pass them on to another. With each step she took, she could feel the weight of the responsibility and she knew she would carry that weight alone.

As dusk began to creep in, Tiger Lily's mind grew silent and she remembered the vision she had in the sweat lodge and the advice of her father. *What would he do?*

Then it came to her, the answer that she had been seeking desperately: *Individually we are strong but together we are unbreakable.*

Tiger Lily knew what she had to do. *I will travel to all the nations and request an alliance, to all come together as one nation against Captain Hook. This will be no easy task, but I have to try.*

Tiger Lily announced her decision to the grand council that she herself would journey to the neighbouring tribes and ask for their presence to battle on the eve of the Great Sun...in return for all of her father's gold.

A wave of objection tore through the meeting.

"That is all our people have left!" bellowed Elder Niikamich "If we give it away, we have nothing."

"If we don't give it away, we run the risk of being destroyed," Peter shot back.

"I cannot agree to this," Elder Niikamich added. "They will never come, not after what happened."

"Nor can I," said another.

"Or I," added another.

"I'm sorry that you all feel so opposed to this decision that I have made, but I assure you. It is what my father would have done, that I know," Tiger Lily asserted. "That is what I am going to put my trust in, and as your leader, this is my final decision."

In the days that followed, Tiger Lily began to assemble provisions for her journey. She would travel inland along the western coast as far as she could, meeting with every tribe along the way. It was suggested by the grand council that she be accompanied inland by Swift Horse and his younger brother, Dancing Crow. They did not want to send out a large party in fear that Captain Hook would hear of her plan. Peter would stay back and protect the village and patrol the waters.

Against Tiger Lily's heart, Pip would remain in the village with Nayhani. Omosseau promised to help care for him while she was away, which gave her great comfort. He would protect Pip with his life if anything were to ever happen while she was away, or if she did not return. As hard as it was to make this decision, she felt it was a sacrifice that came with leadership.

That evening after she announced that she would be leaving little Pip behind, Tiger Lily did not join in around the fire. Instead she left Pip in the care of Nayhani and retreated on horseback to the hot springs several miles from her village. She felt a great sorrow and wanted to be away from the world.

When she arrived at the spring, in the presence of only the moonlight, Tiger Lily removed her garments and slipped into the hot water. She relished in the delight of not feeling so confined in her clothes. She waded about the silky water, sinking deeper into the cloudy mist.

As she lay back in relaxation, she gave herself permission not to worry about the days to come. She allowed herself to believe that the people would come together and she would return safely to little Pip.

In the calm waters beneath the light of the moon, Tiger Lily sat up and gazed at her reflection, hair cascading around her face. *Do I look like my mother?*

Several hours passed before she would emerge from the water. How nice it was to have this time alone. As she was getting dressed, she reached down into her satchel to look for her comb, and there at the bottom of her bag was her headband and her mother's feather that she used to wear so faithfully at the top of her head. She had tucked it away after Jerrekai left because she didn't want it to bend or break during those days and nights she spent hiding in bed with a broken heart.

It had been so long since Tiger Lily's mind wandered to those days, but just like that she was taken back to the memories, back to the vision of the girl who sat on the rock wearing braids and beautifully embroidered clothing watching the young Jerrekai carving flutes and toys. Tiger Lily stared down at the feather, remembering Grandmother braiding her hair and how she would always try to push her away. Now that she was gone, she would give anything to have her braid her hair again.

An enormous sense of gratitude washed over Tiger Lily for the memories the feather carried—and just when she needed them the most. She ran her finger along the ridges and marvelled at its beauty and its strength, and how after all this time, it was still in such immaculate condition. Having it so close to her made her feel protected. But even though the feather brought her great comfort, she knew she could no longer wear it atop her head the way she had before.

Tiger Lily gently removed the feather from the headband and without braiding her hair, tied the quill to a strand of her hair. The feather hung down along the side of her face from the top of her cheekbone and down along her jawline. She walked over to the water to take one last look at herself.

It looks quite pretty, she thought as she stared admirably at the woman in the reflection.

On the horse ride home, the only sounds to accompany her were that of the night wind shaking the leaves in the trees. Tiger Lily breathed in the soft air and drank up the sound of nature as she rode alone in the moonlight. Her mind had come alive and even though she knew that the whole village was probably sound asleep, she was more awake in this moment than she ever was in her life.

Then she wondered about Omosseau, was he up at this hour? She felt so good inside that he was the only person she could think of to share this feeling with. *Do I dare wake him this late?*

As she neared the village, she realized that he had been entering her thoughts quite frequently lately. However, she had been so busy with her planning that she failed to realize that this was not the first time she had had feelings like this.

Then suddenly it became clear, just as clear as the words of her father that were spoken into her heart the day before: Tiger Lily was in love with Omosseau. In that moment as she rode quietly through the woods on horseback, it became evident to her that he had encompassed all of the qualities of everyone that she had ever loved and lost. He was a builder, he was a holy man, he was a leader, he was the giver of wisdom, and he was her friend. He believed in her even when she didn't believe in herself.

Tiger Lily let out a laugh at how funny life was. Just when she had given up on love, when it was no longer in the vicinity of her world...there it was. In the most unlikeliest of disguises—but once revealed, so evident and clear.

"Thank you!" she said out loud. "Thank you." Alone in the dark on her horse, Tiger Lily sent thanks to the Creator and to all her loved ones that had gone on to the spirit world for sending Omosseau to her.

As she rode up to her hut, she wondered how and when she would tell him that she loved him. It would have to be soon, as she was leaving on her journey in the next few days. But when she came up to her doorway, there he was waiting.

"Tiger Lily!" called Omosseau, reaching out to help her down. "I was already beginning to worry, as you have been gone so long. I wanted to come and make sure that you had everything you needed."

Omosseau rambled on as he tied her horse up. He spoke with his head turned and looking down every time they made eye contact. Tiger Lily suddenly realized he was doing this out of respect for her, as she was not dressed in her proper attire. Her hair was still wet and tousled and she wore only a thin night dress that clung to her in the wind and outlined every curve of her body.

Tiger Lily wrapped herself up in a blanket to ease his discomfort.

"I'm sorry." She smiled. "But I'm glad you're here. Please come inside and help me make a fire."

Omosseau built a fire while Tiger Lily put her things away. "Shall I leave until you are finished changing?" he asked.

"I am not going to change," she called out.

"Pardon me?"

"I am not going to change," Tiger Lily repeated herself more quietly as she re-entered the room.

Omosseau lifted his head ever so slightly just enough to notice the movement of her body as she came toward him.

"Can I get you anything else before I leave?"

"The only thing I require this night is your company," revealed Tiger Lily boldly. She leaned in to brush her lips against his, only because she knew that he wouldn't. As great as his affection was for her, his respect was far greater. But that was all the permission Omosseau needed. He took Tiger Lily in his arms and tenderly returned her kiss. Their kiss was long and passionate, and like none that Tiger Lily had ever experienced before.

"I've loved you for a very long time," Omosseau revealed. "But I had to respect your position until you were ready to allow me into your heart."

"I love you too," Tiger Lily confessed. "It just took me longer to realize."

He kissed her again, this time with more fervour and passion than the last. Tiger Lily felt her body go weak from excitement and pleasure as Omosseau's hands left her face and found their way to her waist, pulling her closer and tighter with each deeper kiss.

Tiger Lily embraced him back and the passion became so intense that she had to withdraw herself from him. The sudden shock of all these feelings scared her just a little.

She never felt this much desire and sensation in a single kiss, not even when she experienced her very first kiss.

Omosseau smiled affectionately at her, clearly feeling the same yearning that she was feeling.

"You look beautiful with your hair down," Omosseau said admiringly to Tiger Lily, gently brushing away the stray hairs from the side of her face. "This feather accentuates your beauty."

"This was my mother's feather," she answered. "I wore it all my life. My father gave it to me after she died. He said it would protect me. I don't know why I ever took it off. Maybe I stopped believing it in it."

"You do not believe in it anymore?"

"I don't know," she revealed honestly. "With all that I've been through, I just don't know if I believe that a single item could hold such power. But it does comfort me. It makes me feel that somehow she is with me."

Tiger Lily ran her finger softly down the shaft of her eagle feather, allowing the barbs to tickle her fingertips. "What do you believe?" Tiger Lily asked Omosseau, somewhat apprehensively. She felt almost afraid to hear his answer.

"I feel that the power lies in the belief," he replied. "If you believe that this feather holds the power to protect, then I believe it to be true. I have seen many things unexplained and have even faced death many times and I can only attribute my survival to faith, to a higher power than what you and I can see. We all need something to believe in. It keeps us going when we fear we cannot."

Tiger Lily was relieved that Omosseau did not find her silly to believe that an object such as a feather could protect her. "If ever I were to need her to watch over me, it is now," Tiger Lily divulged. "I really don't know what is out there waiting for me. I've never feared anyone the way I fear Hook, and it is strange—even when he had me tied to a rock and facing death, I did not fear him the way I do right now. Maybe it is because I have little Pip now; I don't want him to grow up without anyone to love him." Tiger Lily felt the tears welling up as she looked over at her young son. "Am I a fool not to have listened to the grand council? Not to move everyone to Neverland? If anything were to happen to the village and little Pip while I am away, I could never forgive myself."

"You are heeding the words of your father in doing what you feel is right, and you are wrong about little Pip. He will never grow up without love because I will be here to make sure of that. Did I ever tell you about my own mother?"

"No," answered Tiger Lily. "Only that she died while you were away."

"When I was a young boy," Omosseau began, "my mother used to catch babies."

Tiger Lily gave Omosseau a puzzled look.

"She would leave some times in the night and when she would return, she would tell us that she went to catch a baby...sometimes two babies. So in my young mind I always envisioned my mother going off into the night and running around in the dark catching babies as they fell from the sky." He laughed. "I didn't realize until I was much older what it meant to catch a baby. I never knew that she was a birthing mom, the only one in our village. I was very proud of her and she was the reason I chose to become a doctor." He smiled lovingly at the memory. "As a boy I would beg her, 'Please, Momma, can I to go help you catch a baby?' My father would always say, 'No! You can't catch babies, only women can catch babies.' When Papa wasn't listening, my mother would whisper in my ear, 'One of these days I will let you catch a baby; I will let you catch your baby.' That night, when I saw your baby being dangled in the air above this cliff, I heard my mother's voice: 'Go catch your baby,' she told me. And I turned my boat around and I caught him as he was falling from the sky."

Tears spilled from Tiger Lily's eyes as she watched the man she loved open his heart to her.

"I have loved your son since the moment he fell into my arms, and I have loved you since the first time I laid eyes on your beautiful face high on the hilltop. So you see, I would never let anything happen to you both as long as there is still breath in my body."

Tiger Lily moved in closer to Omosseau and ran her fingers delicately across his cheek and then down across his jawline. She leaned in and pressed her lips against his, and this time she did not pull away.

CHAPTER 14

A Call to Nations

Two days from now Tiger Lily would leave her village, leave her son, and leave the man she loved to venture off on a journey that she knew deep within was the next right step. But why did she feel so afraid?

"Omosseau, I cannot go," Tiger Lily revealed. "I know I have to but I can't, I can't leave Pip for this long. I just can't!"

"Then we will come with you," Omosseau suggested.

The thought had not crossed her mind that she could take little Pip on this excursion with her. But with Omosseau by her side, Tiger Lily realized he would aid her every step of the way, and not just with little Pip, but with the large task of seeking alliances. Tiger Lily threw herself into his arms. "Thank you, Omosseau, thank you!" she cried. "I would love your company on this trip!"

"Tiger Lily," Omosseau said in a serious tone, "I would like your company for all the days of my life."

She looked up into his glossy eyes as he spoke the sweetest words her ears had ever heard. "Beautiful, strong, courageous woman before me...would you humble my spirit and join your heart forever with mine?"

Tears wet Tiger Lily's cheeks as she stared in silence at the man who had just professed his everlasting love for her. Every breath she took sent waves of happiness throughout her body. She took his head in both of her hands. "I will give you my heart in this life and in the next. I will marry you today."

Tiger Lily, Omosseau, Nayhani, and little Pip made their way to the hill where Elder Blackhorn was dusting off the sweat lodge.

"We have to ask politely," Tiger Lily warned Omosseau in a low voice. "He has refused me many requests in the past."

"Hello, Elder Blackhorn," Tiger Lily said, interrupting his work. "I have come to ask if you will marry us today, as we set sail tomorrow and—"

"No," said Elder Blackhorn before she could finish.

"Why not?" she asked.

"Because I am tired today," he answered plainly and went back to his dusting.

Tiger Lily was insistent. "What about tomorrow? Surely you will be rested by then."

"No," he said, continuing to work without providing any more information.

"Well, why not?"

Elder Blackhorn put down his duster and turned around to face the pair. "You ask for too much!"

Tiger Lily could feel her cheeks turning crimson.

Omosseau opened his coat to reveal a large knife that was carved in a shape that neither Tiger Lily nor Elder Blackhorn had ever seen before. "In my country," he began, "we would carve these weapons out of the tusks of elephants, the largest land creature in the world. Their bones are the strongest of any bone. But there are no elephants here, so I carved this out of your largest sea creature, the whale." Omosseau took the large weapon out of its holder and held it up on front of Elder Blackhorn to display its massive blade and beautifully carved handle.

Elder Blackhorn examined the carvings to find that every animal that was hunted in their lands was skilfully carved into the knife.

"I would like you to take this knife as our offering to you," Omosseau said as he removed the holder from his side and handed it over to Elder Blackhorn. "You are a great man, and have provided many great contributions to your people. We hold you in the highest regard and would be honoured and grateful if you would join us in union under the eyes of the Creator so that we may rightfully share our lives together."

A wide smile spread across Elder Blackhorn's face that, even with almost no teeth left in his mouth, was the brightest smile in the village. "Okay," he beamed. "Let's get married!"

There up on the hill with the afternoon sun settling high into the sky, Omosseau, Tiger Lily, Nayhani, and little Pip became a family.

The excitement of yesterday's events had tired her out tremendously and Tiger Lily fell into a deep sleep, prompting the morning to come seemingly in the blink of an eye.

Omosseau had made a fire and was preparing breakfast. She could vaguely hear him talking about the importance of eating a good meal before a long voyage but her mind trailed off as she allowed her thoughts to become lost in the fire.

As she watched the flames dance, Tiger Lily felt that uneasy feeling begin to re-emerge and she started to question her decision of taking on such a daring endeavour. Her mind became lost in a trance as the methodological sounds of the crackling wood blocked out Omosseau's voice.

What if this doesn't work? What if they do not take me seriously and just come to take the gold and not help? Why should they help me? They will already have their gold! I will become known as the foolish little girl who thought she could fight a war but instead led her tribe to its demise.

She watched the fire dance wildly before her, marvelling at the way the colour of the fire matched the hair on Peter Pan's head. *Oh, how such wonders this great world has created!*

And just then an idea came to her once more, just as clearly as if it had been spoken into her mind: *PETER!*

Tiger Lily jumped up—she needed to see Peter before she left. Omosseau was just about to hand her over a plate of food when she abruptly announced that she needed to leave.

"Omosseau, I'm sorry but I need to see Peter." She spoke quickly, grabbing her shawl. "I cannot travel to these lands and ask these people to follow me into harm's way when I don't know if I can protect them. It seems false to lure someone into danger with gold and treasures. If I do that, I am no better than Hook."

"What are you going to do? We leave today."

"I'm not sure, but I think Peter may be able to help."

All of the village had come to see them off, and with them they brought gifts to bestow on the newly wedded couple. As they rode off on horseback, Tiger Lily looked behind her at all the people waving goodbye and for a moment a dimness had come over her as she was taken back to her youth, to when she boarded the ship with her father as he was taking her away from Jerrekai. She quickly turned away from the crowd of people and looked ahead of her and saw Omosseau riding with Pip. The dark feeling disappeared and she sent a silent thank you in the language of her heart to her father. If she had married Jerrekai, she would never have the love of Omosseau—and more importantly, she would not be mother to her son.

During their long journey, Tiger Lily had ample time to reflect on her life. She thought a lot about her father and what he would say when he approached the tribes. She thought about Iiwatsu and felt sad that he wouldn't get to see his son grow up. She felt guilt that she didn't give him her whole heart in the little time he had on this earth. Then she was reminded of Jerrekai.

He promised her that one day she would find love. The kind of love that he had found, a love she believed didn't exist. Yet it did exist, and she found it. She wished that she could go back to that day in the clearing and say sorry to him and to his bride for all the nasty things she said. *Am I truly deserving of the beauty of this type of love and of this man's heart that belongs to me now?*

When they came upon a rushing river, Tiger Lily dismounted her horse and removed the hand drum she had brought along to play for little Pip at night. She walked to the edge of the water and began to sing a song of honour.

She sang for her people, her family and the nations. She sang a prayer into the wind for Jerrekai and his bride, a prayer of peace and joy and all the blessings of her heart. Nayhani joined her and together they sang for their loved ones listening from the spirit world.

In the days that followed, Tiger Lily, Omosseau, and their small crew visited several nations offering gold in exchange for an alliance. Tiger Lily would present the tribe with an offer of more gold than they had ever seen in their life in exchange for their best warriors to show up and fight on the eve of the Great Sun. She was disheartened at their resistance, though she was not surprised. The last time any of them had visited the Piccaninny village, they brought home death and devastation. How could they ever feel it safe to come back?

But if they felt any of the fear and uneasiness that her tribe felt, Tiger Lily reasoned to herself, they too would want to put an end to Captain Hook and the control he had over the waters. She hoped that offering them a piece of her father's long-admired wealth paired with the possibility that they could be rid of Hook for good would be enough. Though, she also knew that talks of riches and triumph alone would not be enough to get them to risk their lives to fight this extraordinary evil. They needed to believe in Tiger Lily and believe that she was not foolishly leading them to their deaths.

After each seemingly failed meeting, Tiger Lily would lean in to thank each chief with a hug. As they embraced, she would hand off a small scroll and quietly whisper to the chief to read the scroll in secrecy and destroy it immediately after it was read.

When the goodbyes were complete, Tiger Lily and her crew set off to the next tribe, until all the tribes that used the waterways as their main source of transportation and trade had been approached.

Tiger Lily felt guilty for not sharing her plan with Omosseau. She could see that he was worried for her, as she was seemingly failing in her mission. She wanted so desperately to ask him if he thought that the chiefs might actually agree to what she was asking of them in the scroll, but she could not. If she revealed to him what she and Peter and planned the morning of their departure, there was a chance that it could all fall apart.

Similar to the preparation of the potlatch, the village had been busy preparing for the arrival of their guests, though this time without the excitement. People worked to secure safe houses and weapons, and now that Tiger Lily and her crew had returned from their voyage, the work had picked up its pace.

During the grand council meetings, Tiger Lily felt it best not to burden them with details of the cold reception she had received while meeting with the other tribes. If her plan went accordingly, those little details wouldn't matter. But as the eve of the Great Sun fast approached, Tiger Lily could sense the nervousness and anticipation of the tribe as warriors began to arrive, only one or two per nation. *This isn't enough to defend us.*

Tiger Lily tried her hardest to avoid all questions and changed the subject repeatedly when asked about the small numbers. She assured everyone that more warriors were on their way and that they had to remain patient.

Tiger Lily tried to avoid prodding from Omosseau as well. But at night when they were alone, conversation could not be avoided.

"Tiger Lily, I am concerned," said Omosseau, finally working up the courage to shake her confidence. "You haven't been truthful to the others about the meetings."

Tiger Lily pretended not to hear him as she lay still in her bed.

"There is still time..." He paused. "To retreat. There is no shame in failing. But you must act now."

"Omosseau," she whispered. "I feel in my heart that everything will be okay. I just need you to have faith in me."

"Were you with Peter again today?" Omosseau asked, his question unnerving Tiger Lily.

Tiger Lily was aware that Omosseau had made notice of her and Peter engaging in several private conversations over the last few days, and he was politely respecting her privacy. "No, I have not seen Peter in days," she answered.

"I find it strange that your loyal companion is never around in times of crisis...don't you?"

Tiger Lily could hear the annoyance in his voice and she wished that she could ease his mind but she couldn't let him in on her plan. As much as she loved him and relied on him heavily for his wisdom and guidance, Tiger Lily knew this one thing: She could not allow him in. She needed to carry out this plan without him. She just hoped that she could keep him aloof until then without hurting him.

"We need to get some rest," Tiger Lily finally answered him, avoiding his last question.

The Great Sun was drawing near. It was the plan of the grand council to have the women and children go into the safe houses the night before. Nayhani would take little Pip into the house and Tiger Lily was to follow as soon as there were signs of Captain Hook.

Tears flooded Tiger Lily's eyes as she hugged them both and said her goodbyes to little Pip. She knew that if her plan were to fail, there was a chance that this was the last time she would hold him in her arms.

Sombreness filled the air. Just as Omosseau and the council feared, very few other warriors showed up to the battle. They were outnumbered even compared to the numbers they had the night of the first attack at Mermaid's Lagoon.

This fear was enhanced when Peter and the Lost Boys showed up on the shores of the village with news that six pirate ships were spotted lurking nearby. This news was worse than anyone had anticipated. Tiger Lily was thankful that the women and children were already away and did not have to hear this distressing development.

Night was starting to set in on the village as Tiger Lily paced in her hut, attempting to avoid the questions that waited for her if she were to step outside.

"What were you and Peter discussing this evening?" Omosseau asked Tiger Lily.

"Nothing important," she answered dismissively.

"You say that all the time. But your urgency to converse with him would suggest otherwise."

"Omosseau, please!" Tiger Lily huffed anxiously. "Now is not the time to be jealous."

"I feel you pulling away from me at a time where I want to be there for you the most. I am trying to make sense of it."

Tiger Lily knew his observations were true. If only she could ease his heart. But Tiger Lily was fearful; all she could think about was carrying out her plan.

"Omosseau, if something happens to me tonight, promise me you will not stay to fight, but take little Pip and the others and flee far away into the forest."

"What are you talking about?" Omosseau asked, seemingly puzzled by her request. "Why would anything happen to you? You will be with your son."

"I guess I am just afraid, but please, will you do that for me?"

"Of course I will," Omosseau assured her. "Come, I will take you there now."

Tiger Lily allowed Omosseau to walk her to the safe house. They embraced tightly as Tiger Lily allowed a few tears to escape down her cheek. She kissed her husband and watched him disappear into the darkness. But Tiger Lily did not go into the safe house. It was time now to set her plan in motion.

In the dark, Tiger Lily made her way discreetly past the village and down the pathway she had travelled as a young girl. The night air was so quiet that her own brushing through the bushes and the crackling of the twigs beneath her feet scared her. She was terrified of what she may or might not find once she came to the clearing. There on the rock waiting for her was Peter Pan. *This is it! Please, Father, watch over us tonight.*

"I have done what you asked," said Peter in an audaciously loud voice. "I have loaded all of your father's gold onto my ship and we set sail tonight. Captain Hook is in for a surprise tomorrow when he invades your tribe only to find that there is no more gold. By then we will be long gone far away from here, never to be heard from again. I am glad you have decided to come with me so we can start a new life together, just you and me and all our gold!"

"Yes Peter," Tiger Lily called, her tone matching his. "This is what I wanted all along. It has always been you who I loved, you and only you!"

"Come, I have hidden my ship in Footprint Bay. We must go now while it is still dark. It is a long way by rowboat, but by the time anyone realizes we are missing we will be long gone!"

Tiger Lily and Peter scurried down the path together. When they reached the shore, Peter uncovered a small rowboat and urged Tiger Lily to get in.

"Peter, I'm afraid," she whispered.

Peter took Tiger Lily by the hand and gave her a hug. "I know you are," he murmured into her ear. "I'll protect you with my life. But I think the plan is working—the pirates have been following us for days, posing as traders who have lost their way. But I would recognize their snarl anywhere. And I was followed here this night," he assured her, still in an embrace. "We can't back out now."

"Okay." She squeezed him tight. "Let's go."

Tiger Lily climbed into the tiny boat and she and Peter rowed away into the night with their sights set on Footprint Bay.

If only she had turned around to take one last look back toward the village… She may have been able to see her beloved Omosseau staring out after them.

CHAPTER 15

Away in the Night

"Captain, I've prepared your favourite meal," said Mr. Smee, trying to hold the tray steady.

"Get that away from me! Can't you see I'm busy!" growled the captain.

"I will just set it down here for later." Mr. Smee set the tray down on the table as he removed the last tray of untouched food.

Captain Hook had become so consumed with revenge that in these last months, his health had deteriorated rapidly. He rarely ate, slept, or left his bedchambers; his time was spent in his room drafting plans for revenge only to destroy them in a fit of rage if he found even one flaw.

The pirates on board were terrified of him, and avoided him at all costs. When Captain Hook asked them to weigh in on one of his plans, it was a losing game. If the pirates agreed with his plan, he would point out the flaw and then fly into a fit of anger because they agreed to a plan that could lead him into death. And if they didn't agree...well, there was just no disagreeing.

Every pirate was also on strict orders not to kill Peter Pan; anyone attempting such a feat would be tortured for all the days of their life. Peter belonged to the captain, and the captain finally had his plan. A plan that was years in the making and a plan that was meticulously orchestrated and already halfway executed. If anyone spoiled it for him, they would be sorry.

Now that he had weakened the foolish tribe that dared to hide Peter, and rid them of their chief and their sole male heir, he also managed, as a bonus, to instill fear in all the rest of the tribes so that no one would dare get in his way again. Hook was coming for his revenge on Peter Pan, but before he took it, he would strip Peter of all he cared for and Hook would take back all he cared for—his gold and his ship.

It was now time for his plan to come to its climax. It was the eve of the Great Sun, the longest day of the year. The ocean was at its peak and this fervour brought the captain to the height of his own madness.

As planned, Captain Hook had made sure that Peter and the Lost Boys knew that he would attack on this day. He needed to ensure that Peter would be there and not off on some silly adventure. The army of Indian warriors was now weakened so much that Hook no longer feared them and he had now amassed his own army—an army that was not quite skilled in battle but that was feverish for their share of the gold they had all heard the stories about. It was now a waiting game, waiting for the exact right time to strike. As soon as his spies returned, he would have a better idea, but until then his pacing in and out of his room made everyone on board nervous, including Mr. Smee.

"Captain," Mr. Smee called out from the doorway to his bedchambers, "they're back."

"Why are you just standing there? Bring them in!"

The two men scurried inside and immediately removed their hats from their heads.

"Hello Mr. Captain, sir," bumbled the dishevelled-looking man.

"Spit it out! What did you learn?"

"Peter Pan abandoned 'is crew…and da village," the nervous pirate revealed. "He escaped wit da girl."

"Da one 'ose baby yer tossed out into da water," the other pirate interrupted, receiving a scathing look from the other and from Mr. Smee.

"What is he talking about?" the captain asked the first pirate spy.

"It's true," he confirmed. "Pan loaded up yer ship wit da gold. Deys supposed to give it to da peoples who's come ta fight, but he took it and 'id it a few miles from ere. Dey is rowing der now. Dey's planning to run away together. Jus' da two a dem!"

"Hmm… This is better than I expected," the captain said to Mr. Smee. "If you are lying to me I will slice your tongue out," he snapped at the pirates.

"I swear," said the spy.

"What are you going to do, Captain?" asked Mr. Smee. "Our ships are already surrounding the village."

"Well, if it's just the two of them we don't need ships. Are you sure they are alone?" he asked the pirates.

"Yes, not even the Lost Boys is there, they's on land waitin' ta fight."

"Then let's turn this boat around and go after them," Hook yelled excitedly.

"What about the ships?" asked Mr. Smee.

"Let them go to battle. Whoever's left standing will get their reward...if we decide to go back." He smiled. "Come Smee, let's get this ship turned around!"

Captain Hook put his arm around his short companion and led the apprehensive little man up to the ship's wheel. With Captain Hook leading the way, it wasn't long before they spotted a tiny boat off in the distance.

"Peter, I don't see a sign of a ship anywhere. Shouldn't they be following us by now?" Tiger Lily asked nervously.

"I'm sure they will be coming soon, it's still too dark to tell," Peter assured. "But we can't slow down, we need to keep a safe distance between us."

"Oh Peter, what if they aren't there?"

Peter didn't answer immediately, but when he did it was not the answer she wanted to hear. "Then we are rowing to our deaths," he confessed.

Tiger Lily's thoughts immediately went to Omosseau and little Pip. Did she make a mistake not telling Omosseau her plan? What if she was luring herself to her own death—would he ever know that she died trying to save her village and her son?

Tiger Lily looked down at her clenched hands resting in her lap. Inside her palm was the scroll she had given each chief after they had dismissed her pleas for help. In the light of the silvery moon she read over her one last plea to save her home.

Captain Hook has planned to attack our village on the day of the Great Sun. Allow only a small number of your men to travel to the Piccaninny village as requested.

In the highest secrecy, send a band of your greatest warriors to the location on this map several days before the Great Sun. Conceal your boats and wait in the woods near the shores of the eastern bay that is shaped as a footprint.

I will lure Captain Hook into this bay in the wee hours of the morning of the Great Sun. When the signal is released, attack at full force.

Upon my word and the honour of my father, the Chief Great Little Big Panther of the Piccaninny Tribe, you will have your share of ALL his treasures. Tell of this plan to no one, for the future and safety of our villages depend on it.

As the tiny rowboat sailed into the bay, Tiger Lily looked around in the dark. It was eerily quiet. They drifted in silence while only the sound of the waves could be heard. In the chill of the night air, Tiger Lily grew frightened by their solitude. She couldn't shake the terrible thoughts in her mind.

If we go back and fight against Captain Hook and his army, there is no way we can defeat them. Our people don't have it in them to withstand another blow, yet they will fight to the end. We could have been all safe at Neverland right now. Did I make the right choice?

Tiger Lily no longer cared about secret plans and questioning her worthiness; she just wanted to find a way—any way—for her tribe to feel safe and at peace once more. They had withstood so much and had gotten back up each time and continued on, but not without becoming a little more weakened each time. Tiger Lily loved them all, they had become like her children in a sense, and she felt a responsibility to protect them or die trying.

"Tiger Lily, I think I see something," Peter whispered.

Tiger Lily saw it too. There in the darkness... A huge ship had come sailing into their sights, fiercely overpowering and intimidating as it made its way closer to the tiny boat.

Pirates lined both sides of the ship—there were so many of them! As they came closer under the light of the moon, she saw the silhouette of the man who had so many years before orchestrated her capture.

Tiger Lily and Peter sat frozen in the boat looking on as the view of Captain Hook revealed itself more clearly. His hook glinted in the night, and in his other hand was not his usual wide-edged sword, but something large and moving.

Suddenly Tiger Lily let out a piercing scream as she realized what Captain Hook was dangling in front of them. There at his feet was Omosseau bound and gagged.

A roar of hollers came from the woods surrounding the bay. It was the warriors that she had called on! At the sound of her scream, hundreds of them filled the shore line as arrows began to fly past her head and bounce off the side of Captain Hook's ship. Splashes could be heard following the arrows as pirates began to fall lifeless into the water.

"NO! STOP!" screamed Tiger Lily, but it was no use. The battle had begun and she was powerless to stop it.

"Row back to shore," yelled Peter. "It's not safe here!"

"Please, Peter, save him!" she begged, grabbing hold of the oars.

"I'll try my best."

Peter dived off into the water and toward the ship as Tiger Lily rowed her tiny boat out of the way of the flying arrows. She quickly found herself lost amid the swarms of canoes that sailed past her.

When Peter reached the ship, he found there was no way up. He pulled the knife out of his boot and dived beneath the ship. He took his blade and began to gouge holes into the side of the ship in a violent fervour for as long as he could hold his breath.

His impromptu plan seemed to have worked, as the ship began to rise slowly on one side. This was his chance to manoeuvre his way up the sinking side of the ship.

Panting and out of breath, Peter saw his enemy and held up the blade. But just before he was to make his move, two pirates jumped in front of him.

"Leave him!" the captain ordered. The pirates backed away and watched as Captain Hook and Peter squared off.

"Let him go!" Peter called out to Captain Hook, who was still hanging on to Tiger Lily's helpless husband.

"Certainly," said the captain. "I'll need my good hand for this."

In a blast of rage, Captain Hook picked up the large man and threw him over the side of the ship into the water.

Peter dropped his knife and ran in an attempt to jump in after Omosseau, but he was too late—Captain Hook had already grabbed hold of Peter.

Omosseau struggled to break free from the ropes as his head bobbed in and out of the water. But he could not get himself loose and he could feel his strength fading fast. He was no match for the fierce water, and it was tiring him out quicker than he feared. He could not find the strength to call out for help.

In a sudden movement, he was pulled from the water and into a rowboat. As he lay on the dry wooden floor panting and trying to catch his breath, he blinked at the boots of the man who had pulled him into the boat. They were not the shoes of a warrior, but the boots of a pirate. Omosseau sat up in fright and quickly recognized the man sitting across from him.

"Mr. Smee, thank you," he managed to say through his panting. "This is the second time you have spared my life." Omosseau scanned the area around him. The ship was halfway submerged and the warriors were closing in on them. "You must go now," he said to his rescuer. "I am but one man. I cannot protect you from them. Go now! I will swim to shore."

Omosseau stood up and was ready to jump back into the ice-cold waters when he felt a hand on his shoulder.

Mr. Smee locked eyes with Omosseau. "The ships strike at dawn." Then to Omosseau's shock, Mr. Smee dropped his sword and jumped into the water. Omosseau leaned over the side of the rocking rowboat and watched as the plucky aging pirate fought against the waves and the frigid temperatures until he vanished into the dark.

There was no time to waste. The battle between Peter and Captain Hook raged on deck, and he needed to get back to the boat. He picked up the oars and paddled fiercely toward the sinking ship. Before climbing aboard, Omosseau grabbed Mr. Smee's sword and jumped back aboard the ship, dodging tribal warriors' arrows as they continued to zoom by.

There at the head of the ship was Captain Hook standing above a nearly lifeless Peter, who had been disarmed and knocked unconscious. Captain Hook was laughing wildly into the air, triumphant in his pending victory—and unaware that Omosseau was going to derail it.

Omosseau crept in the dark toward the two men, moving quickly now. The captain raised his hook, ready to plunge it into Peter's chest. Omosseau only had seconds to act.

Omosseau lifted up Mr. Smee's sword and, with all of his force and might, plunged the pirate's sword into Captain Hook's back. The thick sharp blade pierced through the velvety coat, into his back and out the other side.

The captain fell to his knees instantly, and his eyes widened at the sight of the bloody sword poking out through his chest. He turned his head to see Omosseau standing over him.

"You fool!" he gurgled. The blood pooled up inside his mouth and his eyes rolled back into his head before they closed for the last time.

The captain's body fell with a hard thud beside Peter Pan. The two men lay side by side —one unconscious, the other dead—as Omosseau and several other pirates looked on.

Omosseau picked up Peter's tiny blade and sliced the captain's throat for good measure. The onlooking pirates watched as Omosseau grabbed the motionless Peter up off the ground and flung him over his shoulder. They cleared the way as the dark man effortlessly carried Peter Pan to the rowboat and rowed him away.

When they were far enough away from the ship, Omosseau dropped the oars and began shaking Peter violently. "Wake up!" But Peter did not respond. In one last effort, Omosseau lifted Peter's limp body over the side of the boat and dunked his head in the frigid water.

Peter shot up out of the water, clamouring for air as a loud roar emerged from the canoes circling the ship. Omosseau looked around. Dozens of canoes of painted warriors cheered, waving their weapons in the air. The ship had completely submerged, taking its slain captain with it.

Amid the roars of triumph, Omosseau could hear his name being shouted. Tiger Lily emerged through the swarm of canoes, pulled her canoe up to his boat, and wasted no time jumping into the vessel. Crying in happiness, she threw her arms around his neck. "You're alive! You're alive!"

"Yes, I am alive," Omosseau assured her, squeezing her close. "I will never leave you."

"I'm so sorry I put you in harm's way," Tiger Lily said. "And I'm sorry I didn't tell you about our plan. I just couldn't let you talk me out of it. I knew you wouldn't let me put my life at risk."

Omosseau grabbed hold of his crying wife and pulled her closer once more. "I would have talked you out of it because I love you so much," he revealed, hugging her tight. "I only ever want your safety."

"Wait!" Tiger Lily shrieked. "Where's Peter?"

"I'm right here," called Peter from the corner of the boat. Still bowled over in pain but now fully conscious, Peter managed a smile to show Tiger Lily that he was okay.

She flung her arms around Peter's neck, oblivious to his yelps of pain. "It worked, Peter! Our plan worked!"

Peter managed to laugh through his pain as Omosseau helped him to his seat.

Omosseau looked around and could see everyone clearly. Mr. Smee's words rang in his ears: "*They attack at dawn.*"

"We have no time to spare!" he yelled. "The pirates are still surrounding the village; they will attack at dawn!"

Tiger Lily stood up in the boat and yelled out her order. "This is not over yet! There are pirates surrounding the village! We have to go now!"

A large sound of cheers rang through the air. Scores of men in dozens of canoes started paddling toward the Piccaninny shores.

Tiger Lily was too anxious to sit. With every breeze that brushed across her face, she sent a prayer into the wind, into the ears of her father, her mother, her grandmother, Nascha, and her dear Iiwatsu, praying that she and the others would make it in time.

She squinted into the horizon, trying to make out shapes in the rising predawn light. Just as Omosseau warned, there were five large ships closing in on the shores of the Piccaninny Tribe. The nervousness rose up through her chest but then she shoved the fear aside. She was not alone in this battle to save her people.

Chief Red Eagle called out his signal, and within moments the men lined their canoes side by side. He gave a second call, and in unison, fire blazed across the tips of their arrows pointing to the sky.

Chief Red Eagle stood in his boat, fist in the air to give his final command. When his fist dropped, dozens of arrows were released into the air in an array of tiny fireballs heading straight toward the pirate ships. Again the call was made and another round of flaming arrows shot into the air, and again and again and again.

Tiger Lily gasped with a mixture of fear and wonder. Could they win this battle?

The ships became engulfed in flames as pirates started jumping into the water. Tiger Lily watched from her tiny rowboat as the Piccaninny warriors, the Lost Boys, and the initial tribal warriors ran out on to the shore and into their boats to stop the pirates from making their way onto land.

It was over. The pirates were rendered helpless and had been overcome. It was all over. Tiger Lily collapsed into her husband's arms as Peter cheered at the sight of this victory.

The Great Sun was up and Tiger Lily could now see the tremendous number of canoes that filled the shores.

As she looked around at all the handsomely painted warriors, she noticed at once that not only had the chiefs sent their best men, but they too had come to fight. Her heart exploded with pride.

CHAPTER 16

Still Waters

True to her word, Tiger Lily disbursed all of Chief Great Little Big Panther's gold among the tribes. New alliances had been formed and the threat of Captain Hook was gone forever. To the Piccaninny Tribe, the value of safety and security was worth more than any amount of gold in the world. They were more than happy to hand it over to their new friends.

As the tribe waved off the last of the canoes in gratitude, Tiger Lily felt a bit of sadness creep over her joyous spirit; the departure of the last tribe meant the forthcoming departure of another. Peter and his Lost Boys had decided that they would be moving on to a new adventure, yet this time with no promise of return.

The tribe felt this as a great loss, but none more so than Tiger Lily. Peter had become family to her, someone she had grown to depend on to feel safe and protected. But since she no longer needed protection and she now had her own family to fill her void of loneliness, she needed to release Peter from any obligation to her and her tribe.

She knew that he would stay as long as she needed him to, but in her heart she knew that Peter's adventurous spirit needed to be free to roam and explore. He was never meant to stay in one place for so long, and Tiger Lily was grateful that she had his devotion and support for all these years. It was time now to say goodbye.

The ceremony for Peter and the Lost Boys felt just like old times. There was feasting, dancing, singing, and laughing. It carried on well into the night as the tribe reminisced around the fire and retold stories of their recent victory.

When morning came, Peter and his Lost Boys docked their ship and came on shore for one last goodbye.

One by one, the grand council members went down the line and said their formal goodbyes, presenting gifts to each of the boys. Omosseau gifted each Lost Boy with his own carved knife that he worked on day and night leading up to this morning.

When it came time for Tiger Lily to say goodbye, she went down the line with little Pip and Nayhani at her side and presented each of the boys with a sacred eagle feather. But when she came to Peter, Tiger Lily could no longer hold back her tears. She embraced her friend and allowed her tears to wet his shoulders. "You will always have a place around our fire, and Neverland will always be your home," she spoke softly into his ear.

Peter squeezed her tight and then bent down to say goodbye to little Pip and Nayhani. When he stood back up to face Tiger Lily, she told him she too had a gift for him.

Tiger Lily carefully removed the eagle feather that was tied to her flowing hair and ran her fingers gently across the barbs of the white and brown feather one last time.

"May this feather guide and protect you on your journey the way you have guided and protected all of us," Tiger Lily said as she lovingly placed her mother's feather upon the brim of Peter's cap.

"Tiger Lily, I can't... It's your mother's feather," objected Peter.

"Yes you can," she assured him. "I no longer need the protection this feather has provided me with, but you, my friend, have many more adventures to come."

"Thank you," Peter whispered, mirroring her glassy gaze.

Elder Blackhorn sounded his drum and the entire tribe began to sing the Piccaninny honour song as Peter and his men boarded their ship.

"Do you think he will ever be back?" Nayhani asked Omosseau.

"Yes, I believe he will be back," Omosseau assured her. "This is the only home Peter has ever known. It may not be to stay, but we will see him again."

Until we meet again, dear friend. The last of Tiger Lily's tears trickled down her cheeks as she and the others watched their dear friend sail over the horizon and out of sight. So many people had come and gone so quickly from her life and it saddened her to be losing another.

It was a wonderful feeling to know that there could be love without fear as days turned into years and huts became homes. Joy and laughter found its way back into their community and life blossomed all around them.

Omosseau and Tiger Lily had welcomed two more sons and a daughter into their family—Omassai, after Omosseau's father, Raigon, and Nascha Bear. Each new day brought new smiles to their faces and new adventures to be navigated together. Tiger Lily was amazed at how much love a heart was able to contain, and it was in these moments of sentiment that she would think of her father.

Tiger Lily could now fully understand how the unhappiness of someone you love could consume you. It was also in these quiet moments that her thoughts would sometimes wander to Captain Hook, for he too was once an innocent loving child. Whatever could have happened in his life that could cause him to become so damaged that he would grow to be a man with no remorse or conscience?

Looking now at her own children, so happy and pure, Tiger Lily felt sad for the young boy pictured in her mind who grew up to learn hate.

As she sat on the rock in the clearing of her youth, Tiger Lily joyously watched as Omosseau carved out flutes for their children.

"You like this spot, don't you?" Tiger Lily smiled at her husband, who was helping Pip carve his first flute. The other children watched in fascination as the willow changed its shape with every slice of the knife.

"It has the best willow around," answered Omosseau, turning his answer into a lesson for the children. "The willow in this clearing grows closest to the sun and is nourished by all this fresh air."

"Are you sure it is not because this is where we first met?" Tiger Lily asked playfully.

Omosseau smiled. "Meeting you on this cliff was the day my life truly began," he said, his eyes shining with love. He dug into his pocket and pulled out three small flutes for the children and took a seat next to Tiger Lily to watch the children fill the air with toots and whistles.

Tiger Lily felt a lump form in her throat as she hugged her husband. "Do you ever still wish that you could go home?" she asked him.

"I am home," Omosseau said matter-of-factly. "Sometimes I dream about my village in Africa and my people and the friends that I left behind, but they are all gone now. You and our children are home to me, and wherever you are is where I am content to be."

Tiger Lily knew what he meant because she felt the same way. She still had her village but Omosseau and her children were *home*. As she turned to look out over her shoulder at the vast dark blue sea, Tiger Lily thanked all who loved her long ago and for the strength they gave to her. Then she looked at her children and thanked them for the love and strength they provided her with today and each day to come. A smile spread across her face as she watched them run about playfully in the clearing, as her youngest tried to keep up with the boys, her wild curly hair blowing in the wind.

ABOUT THE AUTHOR

Jill Featherstone (pseudonym) is a Cree/Ojibway Author, University Professor, motivational speaker, workshop facilitator, blogger and proud wife, mother & grandmother from the Misipawistik Cree Nation in northern Manitoba, Canada. She holds a Bachelor's Degree in Education and a Master's Degree in Guidance and Counseling. In 2013 she founded Featherstone Support Services to provide motivational workshops for Indigenous youth and young adults.

"Empowering Indigenous young people is always at the forefront of whatever I am doing, and whether it's through writing, workshops, speaking, or social media, I am always in search of ways to reach people on a larger scale." To learn more about Jill or subscribe to her blog, visit www.jillfeatherstone.com.

In 1929 author J.M. Barrie gifted the Great Ormond Street Hospital Children's Charity the rights to Peter Pan. Although the copyright has since expired and does not apply to sequels and spin-offs, Jill Featherstone has taken inspired action and pledged to donate a percentage of the royalties to various Indigenous Youth Leadership initiatives.